THE TIME OF THE LAWMAN

From the plains of Southern Nebraska, down to the deserts and high ranges of Nevada, was some journey for a man with a pack of lawmen on his trail. But even reaching Nevada did not mean the end of the trail for Rob Gardner. Several men had fallen out from the posse hunting him down, but Rob knew that nothing would stop the hard and ruthless Jeb Harbinger. With nowhere else to run, Gardner stood his ground, strangely unafraid and with a gun in his steady hand. The hunted suddenly became the hunter . . .

ALAN P. VINSON

THE TIME OF THE LAWMAN

Complete and Unabridged

LINFORD
Leicester

First hardcover edition published in
Great Britain in 2003 by
Robert Hale Limited, London

Originally published in paperback as
The Time of the Lawman by Chuck Adams

First Linford Edition
published 2005
by arrangement with
Robert Hale Limited, London

British Library CIP Data

Vinson, Alan P.
   The time of the lawman.—Large print ed.—
Linford western library
1. Western stories
2. Large type books
I. Title II. Adams, Chuck
813.5′4 [F]

ISBN 1–84395–608–X

Published by
F. A. Thorpe (Publishing)
Anstey, Leicestershire

Set by Words & Graphics Ltd.
Anstey, Leicestershire
Printed and bound in Great Britain by
T. J. International Ltd., Padstow, Cornwall

This book is printed on acid-free paper

1

Wolf Pack

They came riding slowly down out of the darkness of the moonlight night, with the shoulders of the high hills sloping downward around them on both sides, clamping towards the dim, twisting trail where the cold breeze funnelled without cease, bearing to them the smell of sage and pine. They had found a camp some three miles back and had wasted precious moments quartering it, in case the man they sought was still there, lying in wait for the first of them to place his unwary head where it could be sighted by the notched V of a Winchester. But the fire was dead, the ashes grey and there were signs of a solitary man having sat there some unguessable time before, but nothing to indicate whether he was the man they wanted or not.

Now they rode in a tight bunch behind the tall, hard-faced man who rode the black sorrel, head lifted in spite of the wind that grew stronger as they progressed until it whipped tears from their half-closed eyes and uptilted the rims of their hats, filling the air with a thin, stinging dust that bore traces of abrasive, caustic alkali on its breath.

The further they rode on to the stretching plains, the wilder grew the night, with a storm beginning to rumble over the high peaks at their back, and an occasional forked flash of distant lightning which crackled across the heavens, lighting everywhere in a steel-grey second.

Gloved, dust-layered from the long trail, their horses moved with a growing weariness until they suddenly scented water in the distance and quickened their loping pace a little, forcing their flagging feet onward.

They had left behind the wide plains of Nebraska and less than twenty miles ahead of them lay the great Sangre de Cristo mountains of Colorado; and still the man they hunted was somewhere ahead of them. They had raised his scent on one or two occasions on the border, but had then lost him. Had they been able to make their own decision, there was no doubt that the men of the posse would have given up there and then, turned back and returned to Nebraska, content in the knowledge that they had ridden as far as the law permitted, that they had no jurisdiction outside of the State and that they had assured themselves that Rob Gardner had been ridden out of the territory.

But any suggestion like that had been immediately overruled by the brute of a man who rode on now in the lead, heading to God knew where, filled only with the determination to hunt down the man he sought, and kill him. His name was Jeb Harbinger, a tall, thick-set man, heavy jowled, with sharp eyes which had a way of looking at a man as if daring him to go for his gun.

The hands which held the heavy reins were broad, matted with hairs on the backs, blunt-fingered; and his head rolled a little on his broad shoulders with the motions of his mount.

Another mile and he suddenly held up his right hand to stop the posse. They paused at the curve of a dry wash where a stream had once run down the hillside, but where only a dried-up bed of white, polished, sun-bleached stones now marked out its former course.

His sharp-eyed gaze singled out one of the men in the darkness. He said tautly: 'You, Condon. You know this stretch of territory. How far are we now from any town?'

'Another two hours yet, Marshal. Hard ridin'.'

'This trail lead to it?'

'That's right. Connaught. Nothin' much there, just a leftover from the days of the Gold Rush in these parts. May be deserted now.'

'We'll head there anyway,' said Harbinger, making up his mind at once.

4

'He could've headed that way.'

'You reckon that was his camp we found, Marshal?' asked Sutton. 'If it was, that camp could have been more'n ten days old.'

'Could be. If he started out over this desert, the chances are he won't stop until he hits the Sangre de Cristo range.'

'Those mountains are all of a hundred and fifty miles long and he won't find it easy gettin' over 'em at this time of year. The snows will be meltin' and every river will be in flood there.'

'Maybe so, but when a man knows he's got a posse on his trail, he'll try anythin',' grunted Harbinger. He turned in the saddle. 'Let's move. We've got distance to cover and that storm is gettin' close.'

Thunder rode with them through the lightning-splintered darkness. Now the ground was as level as a table, with all of the hardness and the emptiness hidden for a while by the night.

Harbinger stared out from beneath lowered brows. Colorado was a thousand miles of desert and mountains, flatness and sheer rising savagery, as if the entire earth had been caught up and tilted on edge, great rocks lifting sheer into the heavens. Mostly it was waterless and sterile, covered with a fine dust that got into a man's clothing, worked its way next to the skin and hurt his hide with its itching, burning irritation. Ten days on the trail in Colorado had been more than enough to convince him that there was nothing here which would tempt him and if anything, the country would get worse before they reached the end of this particular trail. Gardner had several days' lead on them and the men who rode with him were beginning to lose heart for this particular job. But there would be no turning back until he had come face to face with Rob Gardner and killed him. Even if the men at his back fell out one by one on the trail, he would go on alone, would destroy this man who had broken the law. Not once, during the whole of his career as a Marshal had any man escaped from him. It always had been his proud boast that any man he hunted down came back across his own saddle, another candidate for Boot Hill. He had sworn that the same thing would happen with Rob Gardner and nothing this side of hell was going to stop him from fulfilling that oath.

Right and left of them, the crumpled hills fell further and further away. Then, almost two hours later, they topped a low rise and stared down at the dark shadow that sprawled in front of them, a few yellow lights sprinkled in the black mass of buildings.

'There's Connaught,' said Condon, pointing. 'Guess I was wrong about it bein' deserted. Some kind of life down there, anyways.'

Harbinger nodded, but said nothing. 'We'll take a look,' he said harshly.

They rode down the gentle slope and into the main street of Connaught. The riotous night life of the town seemed to be in full swing and Connaught looked anything but a ghost town, although several of the houses on the outskirts looked distinctly unsafe, with their walls and roofs collapsing slowly with every passing year. Harbinger loosened one holstered gun and let his hand rest gently on it, prodding his horse forward along the dusty, shadowed street, the lights on either side tracing out the dusty highway that ran straight through the town. There were one or two men standing on the boardwalks and Harbinger was mindful of eyes that watched them curiously as they rode by.

There was scarcely a sound to be heard now above the soft noise of hoofs on the road. The thunder had moved off to the north, skirting the town and only a faint rumble added to, rather than detracted from, the utter stillness. But in spite of the silence, there was not that feeling in the night that a wary man could sense, the feel of an itch in the small of the back, or the crawling of tiny hairs on the nape of the neck. Leaving their horses in front of the saloon, the posse moved inside and only Harbinger remained in the street for a few moments longer, before heading in the direction of the Sheriff's office, where a pale yellow light still gleamed through the dust-covered window that looked out on to the boardwalk.

Thrusting open the door, he stepped inside. There was a man seated behind the desk, his legs on top of it, eating from a bowl. The other's head came up alertly, eyes widening a little at the sight of a stranger walking in like this, at this late hour of the night.

Placing the bowl on the desk, the other wiped his mouth with the back of his hand, then swung his legs off the top of the desk and got slowly to his feet.

'Howdy, Marshal,' he said quietly, glancing at the star on the other's shirt, where his heavy coat and jacket swung open slightly as he moved forward. 'You just ridden into town?'

Harbinger nodded. 'That's right. You the Sheriff here?'

'Nope, I'm just the deputy. Sheriff Crowder is over at the saloon. Want me to fetch him for you?'

Harbinger pondered that for a moment, then shook his head. 'Guess I'll go across and find him,' he said quietly. 'I need somethin' to wash the trail-dust out of my throat.'

'You'll find him in the Trail's End, Marshal.' The other came to the door and pointed to the saloon a little further along the street and on the opposite side. Harbinger gave a brief nod, untethered his mount and walked it across to the saloon. He bent to ease the cinch, then walked up the sagging steps and through the swing doors into the glare of the saloon where the flickering yellow light of the lanterns danced around the walls and found sharp reflection in the long crystal mirror which backed the bar itself.

There were men at the round tables and along the edge of the carved hardwood bar but at first, he could see nothing of a man with a star on his chest. Then he bent his glance further from the bar, saw a table set back from the light of the lamps, saw the short, hatchet-faced man who sat there, the glint of metal whenever he moved his arm so that the short waistcoat lifted a little to reveal his shirt. There was another man with him, tall and thin to the point of gauntness and both looked up as he moved across and stood in front of the table, near the empty chair.

'Sheriff Crowder?' Harbinger asked quietly.

The short man nodded, eyes narrowed a little. It did not take too much study to come up with a fairly accurate appraisal of the other. He belonged to the usual breed of men who took on the job of lawman in a town like this, a man who tried to be honest, but who knew that he would not keep his job for long if he went against the men who had put him where he was. In Connaught, Harbinger reckoned, that would be the

11

bankers or the cattlemen. Not a strong enough character to enforce the law impartially, with neither fear nor favour.

Crowder on the other hand, knew that the man who faced him was trouble four ways come Sunday, his eyes taking in the tied down guns, the deep-set eyes and the sucked-flat mouth. For a moment, he even considered that he had seen this man's face on a wanted poster in his desk drawer. Then he dismissed the idea at once as the other said: 'Mind if I talk with you for a moment, Sheriff. In private. The name is Harbinger, United States Marshal.'

Crowder drew in a thin hiss of air, flicked a quick glance at his companion, who quickly got to his feet, scraping back his chair and backing away from the table with a mumble of something under his breath. Then Crowder glanced back at Harbinger. 'Sit down, Marshal,' he said, his tone a trifle too high-pitched to be his usual voice. 'Never figured we'd have you ride in here. What's on your mind? Lookin' for somebody on the run?'

'That's right. Have you had a rider through here any time in the past ten days? Tall, twenty-five or so, dressed in black range clothes.'

Harbinger could hear some of the men stirring at his back, knew that they had temporarily given up their cards, were watching him closely, their stares on him from behind.

'Within ten days, you say,' murmured Crowder musingly. He ran a finger down one side of his nose. 'Could be that you and me are lookin' for the same man, Marshal.'

For a moment, a hardness came to Harbinger's face and his eyes drew down to mere slits as he regarded the other without moving. 'Maybe you could explain that, Sheriff,' he said.

The other's features were briefly impassive. He shrugged. 'A couple of men rode into town eight days ago. Both were strangers and it was obvious they had ridden some distance. About two hours after they got here, the stage came in. Sam Devlin the man ridin' shot gun had a couple of slugs in his shoulder, and the strongbox was gone. Seems they'd been held up by two masked men six miles out of town. I got myself a posse together and we rode to the spot, found sign there but not enough to allow us to track 'em through the desert.'

'So you figured those two *hombres* who rode into town ahead of the stage might have been the men?'

'We checked, naturally, but they didn't have the bullion box.'

'It wouldn't have been difficult for them to have hidden it somewhere between where they held up the stage and Connaught.'

'I guess not. But I don't have enough men to send 'em out on a wild goose search like that. I reckoned I could keep an eye on those two critters so long as they stayed in town. I had three men watchin' the hotel, just to make sure they didn't slip out, pick up the strongbox and ride out with it.' Sheriff Crowder began making a smoke. He went on a trifle resentfully: 'They made their try four days ago. One of 'em slipped out through a window while the other made sure my men saw him inside the room.'

'And your men fell for the trick?'

Crowder's answer was slow in coming but eventually he admitted: 'We got the man in the room, but by the time we found out what had happened to the other, he was out of town and miles away. There are a dozen trails he could've taken in the darkness. It was senseless tryin' to track him down.'

Harbinger lit a thin black cheroot, regarded the sullen red tip for the briefest fraction of a second, then stared back at the other. Hesitating for a moment, he dug deep into his jacket pocket, came up with a folded piece of paper, passed it to the sheriff. 'Take a look at that man and tell me if he was one of these two *hombres*.'

Crowder lit up, exhaled a cloud of

bluish smoke, wagged his head a little as he unfolded the paper and spread it out with his hands in front of him on the table, bending forward to peer down at the picture in the dim light. Then he looked up, nodded his head slowly. 'That's the coyote who got away, and on a stolen horse too, sure as God made little green apples, Marshal.'

Harbinger let out a faint sigh from between tightly-clenched teeth. He took the picture back, folded it carefully along the original crease lines and replaced it in his pocket, then drew deeply on his cheroot. Inwardly, he felt tense and restless, knowing that the man he hunted was only four days' travel ahead of him at the most. He wanted to be on his way again, to drive the men in the posse to the very limit of their endurance, knowing that he could keep on riding through the night and all of the next day too if the necessity, the driving force, was there. But a moment's reflection told him that the others would refuse to go any further that night. They did not have this desperate, inner urge to catch up with Rob Gardner. It was of little real consequence to them if they caught him or not. Already, he had heard some of them grumbling about this ride which seemed destined to take them across half a dozen states of the Union before they caught their man. He knew, too, that some of them were a little unsure of the legal position, of whether they had a right in law, to operate outside of Nebraska. Already, they were hundreds of miles from their home territory and with each day that passed, they thought a little less of why they were riding with him, and a little more about returning home to their wives and families. Yet he meant to drive them on to the very end of this trail. The desire to come face to face with Gardner, to shoot him down, in a fair fight or in the back, was so strong within him that it was something he could not fight down, something growing more powerful and irresistible every hour. No man had fallen foul of

Marshal Jeb Harbinger and got away with it; that was his reputation and he intended to keep it intact, no matter what it cost.

He turned his head to assess the feelings of the men in the saloon, the vague, faint night noises which drifted in through the doors that looked out on to the street.

'The man you caught,' he said thoughtfully. 'Where is he now?'

'Why in jail, of course,' said the other, mildly surprised. 'I got him locked up ready for trial next week.' He sat there, briefly silent, as he drew on his smoke, brows pulled tightly together in a faint scowl. 'You want to question him about his pardner? If so, I reckon you ought to do it as soon as possible. There ain't no doubt what the verdict is goin' to be when he's tried, and we'll string him up real fast, soon as Judge Kenner has pronounced sentence. We don't allow slow justice here.'

'Somehow, I don't reckon he'll talk that easy, even if he knows anythin'' about my man. This *hombre'* — he tapped his jacket pocket where the picture now reposed — 'was travelling alone when we last came across one of his camps. I figure he must've just met up with this other critter and they both decided to rob the stage.'

'Why should they do that, perfect strangers.' Crowder polished the badge on his shirt with his sleeve, and swung his eyes restlessly right and left as if expecting to find the answer to that question somewhere in the saloon around him.

'I don't know. It could be I'll find the answer from this man you have in your jail.'

'All right. I'll take you over to see him. But don't expect him to be co-operative. He hasn't answered any of our questions. I don't see how you can make him change his mind, not when he knows he's goin' to hang for sure, no matter what he does or says.'

Getting to his feet, he crossed over the saloon, angling among the tables, until he reached the doors and thrust them open with the flat of his hand. He felt a little uncomfortable about the presence of the man who followed so close at his back, felt a tiny shiver go through him, similar to that which he had experienced when the other had first told him who he was. Marshal Jeb Harbinger! There was scarcely a man in the whole of the territory who had not heard that name at some time or other. From what Crowder had heard, the other had certainly earned his name as the Killer Marshal; a hard, utterly ruthless man, whose idea of upholding the law was to hound down any man he considered to have broken it, to follow him from one end of the country to the other if needs be. And always, he brought in his man dead, across his own saddle. It seemed to give the other some kind of fiendish pleasure to kill every man he hunted. He had never been known to bring in a prisoner alive for trial by judge and jury. The Colt was, for him, sufficient judge and jury to enable his kind of rough, range justice to be carried out to the letter.

The trouble was, that there had been talk at times that some of the men he had hunted down and killed had subsequently been proved to have been innocent of the charges Harbinger had brought against them. It did not seem likely that this was the case as far as the man Gardner was concerned. After all, was it not undoubtedly true that he had helped in the robbing of the stage? He may also have been the one who had shot the guard. Still, he would not like to be in Gardner's shoes now, even though the other probably had four days lead on Harbinger.

Entering the office, he slitted his eyes against the orange glow that came from the stove in the corner where three men were lounging against the wall, two with Winchesters balanced in the crooks of their arms. Harbinger gave them a quick glance, wondered if the deputy had brought them in as soon as he had gone over to the saloon seeking the sheriff.

'Just got the coffee on, Sheriff,' said one of the armed men. 'Be ready in a couple of minutes if you'd like some.'

'Thanks. Better get a cup for the marshal too. He's had a long ride today. He'll probably be needin' it more'n me.'

'Sure thing, Sheriff.'

Without pausing, Crowder led the way along a short passage, to the cells at the rear of the building. Harbinger followed close on the other's heels, let his gaze drift over the steel-barred front of the nearest cell. Within this meshed cage, a man lay humped on the low bunk, sleeping with an old Army blanket thrown over him.

'Let me have the keys, Sheriff,' Harbinger said, holding out his hand. There was a distinct trace of impatience in his voice.

Crowder hesitated, then handed them over, watched stoically as the marshal opened the cell door, stepped inside, and crossed over to where the prisoner snored loudly under the blanket. Bending, he shook the other awake roughly.

The man opened his eyes, came swiftly awake, but did not move. He had the air of a hunted animal about him as he stared upward, fully alert, yet there was something else, a look of cunning at the back of his eyes, that Harbinger recognized at once.

'What's your name, mister?' Harbinger asked harshly. He still retained his tightly-clenched grip on the other's shoulder.

For a moment, it seemed the other did not intend to answer, then he must have seen something in the marshal's face, for his eyes widened a little, his tongue flicked out to wet his dry lips, and he said tightly: 'Frenchy Vereau.'

Harbinger's lips twitched into a faint smile, but there was no mirth in it. Mirth was also absent from his voice as he said: 'That's a change from Smith, I reckon, but just as false.'

The other swung his legs to the floor, shook off Harbinger's restraining hand, then said harshly: 'Just why are you askin' me questions? What's this to do with you? You just another of Crowder's sidekicks?'

Harbinger straightened. He looked grim and sardonic now. 'You know somethin' that I intend to find out, Vereau,' he muttered. 'If my name means anythin' to you, it's Jeb Harbinger.'

'Marshal Harbinger!' The other's tone was proof enough, if any were needed, that he had heard of this man who now faced him in the dimness of the cell. He turned his eyes on the other. 'This is no concern of yours, Marshal. So long as I'm here in jail, I come under the Sheriff's jurisdiction and — '

'I'm not interested in you, Vereau. They'll hang you in a few days anyway. But I want to know about the other man who was with you. Where he is, how you met him, what part he had to play in robbing the stage — and if he was the one who shot the stage guard. He was, wasn't he?' There was an odd intensity in the marshal's tone as he asked the last question. It was almost, thought Sheriff Crowder, standing near the door of the cell with his hand close to the butt of the Colt in his belt, as if he were putting these words into the other's mouth, giving him a let-out on the charge of shooting the guard. Not that it made any difference to what would happen to Frenchy Vereau, but it would give him another charge to press against the man he was hunting.

'Why sure, Marshal. He shot the guard. I just wanted to hold up the stage without any shootin'. Would have done it too, if it hadn't been for that hot-headed young fool. Had to use his gun even when there were no reason for it.'

'You sure of that, Frenchy?' Crowder broke in. 'I heard different from the stage driver. He claimed it was you did the shootin'.'

'I'll do the questioning here, Sheriff,' Harbinger said tersely, swinging on the other. 'I know the kind of man Rob Gardner is. It fits with his reputation as a gunslinger and killer.'

'Gardner?' Vereau's lips thinned in a mirthless grimace. 'That ain't the name he gave me when we planned to hold up the stage. Said his monicker was Thatcher.'

'Then you admit you did hold up the stage?'

'Reckon there ain't no sense in denyin' it,' grunted the other sullenly.

'Then maybe you'll explain why you planned it with a man you only knew for a day, a stranger, who might have been a lawman for all you knew.'

The other leaned against the wall, near the small, square window eyeing his hands reflectively. Then he said scornfully: 'It was his idea, Marshal, his from beginning to end. It sounded good when he put it up to me and I agreed to throw in with him. Now leave me be, Marshal. There ain't any more I can tell you.'

'He's run out on you, Vereau, left you to face swingin' from the end of a rope while he digs up the strongbox from where you buried it and heads out of the territory. Do you think he's worried about what will happen to you?'

'Damnit to hell, Marshal. I know what he's done. But you don't have to worry none on my behalf. He'll be back with some of the boys from the hills and I'll be out of this stankin' jail before you know what's hit this town.'

Harbinger shook his head slowly. 'You're wrong, Vereau. You don't even know this *hombre*. But I do. I've been trailin' him with a posse since he left Nebraska some weeks ago. I don't aim to rest until I've run him to earth and shot him dead — and he knows it. He won't come back for you. He's too busy tryin' to keep one jump ahead of me. Maybe though, that money you took from the stage is goin' to help him to stay in front of me just a little longer than otherwise; unless you get wise to the fact that he's just used you, and tell me where he's headed. Then I can promise you, I'll see that he swings too.'

'How should I know where he's headed? There are a hundred trails around Connaught and he could have taken any one.'

'I doubt that,' said the marshal evenly. His face tightened just a shade. 'You must've laid some plans for when you got out of town and picked up the money. Nobody plans to rob a stage of twenty thousand dollars, and leaves it just at that. They always go one step further and plan where they mean to split up after they've shared out the loot.' His smile was as cold as his words.

'I don't know anythin' about that,' muttered the other sullenly.

'No?' Harbinger's face changed abruptly. 'You know which trail he meant to take, and I mean to get that information from you by any means I have to use.' His words fell like stones down a deep muffling well. 'It's up to you whether we do this the hard way, or you tell me right now.'

A hard wrath seemed to grip him, to swell the curving veins in the bull-like neck, drawing a thin film over the deep-set eyes. His hand snaked out, caught the other's shirt, bunching it in his grip as he hauled the man close to him, thrusting his face up to Vereau's.

'You'd better tell me,' he said ominously, 'otherwise they won't need a hangin' party for you.'

Vereau licked his lips. It was obvious the type of man he was; brave when in company with others of his own kind, but a craven coward when he was alone, facing trouble like this. His courage deserted him now. He had never come up against a man like this, and he too had heard of the Killer Marshal.

'He's headin' for the Sangre de Cristo mountains. There's a pass over them which should be open even at this time of year. Most others will be snowed up but this should be open.'

'You know where this pass is?'

The other nodded. 'A couple of days' ride from here, south-west. There's a trail leads off to it a day and a half from Connaught.'

'Thanks.' Harbinger turned away just as one of the armed men came along the corridor, pausing outside the door of the cell. 'Coffee's ready, Marshal,' he said, glancing from the sheriff to Harbinger, then back again, a faintly puzzled look on his face.

Harbinger stepped out of the cell, turned for a moment to where Vereau had made a smoke, was lighting it with a hand that shook a little. The outlaw glanced through the bars of the cell at him, then let his look slide away, as if afraid of what he saw there, mirrored on the other man's face and in his eyes.

Seated in a chair near the hot stove, Harbinger drank down the coffee in quick gulps. The night outside had been cool, especially after they had ridden down from the wind-swept hills and the fire here was warm. He let the heat soak into his back and chest, relaxing the taut muscles that had been drawn hard and tight through his body.

'You get everythin' you wanted out of Vereau?' asked Crowder at length.

Harbinger rolled a second cup of coffee between the palms of his hand, before nodding. 'We'll ride out tomorrow at sun-up,' he said. 'You reckon the hotel could put us up for the night?'

'I guess so. We don't usually get as many men in town at one time, but I figure there ought to be room enough, if some of the men don't mind sleepin' two to a room.'

'I reckon not,' Harbinger grinned mirthlessly. 'They've all slept rough on the trail before now. They won't mind this for one night.'

Inside his room at the hotel, Harbinger took off his gunbelt and laid it carefully on the small wooden table beside the iron bed, took off his heavy jacket and placed it over the back of the chair. There was a deep weariness in his limbs which he tried in vain to fight down. The hot coffee he had drunk in the sheriff's office had temporarily acted as a stimulant, but now the effect was beginning to wear off. When a man rode a long trail, there were times when he had to stop and ask himself why he was doing it. Most of the men he had hunted down in the past had ridden for perhaps a couple of days before he had run them to earth. It had been easy to keep a posse together then. But now it was going to be different. How many of these men would stick with him if they were forced to go on for another ten or twenty days, through the pass over the top of the high Sangre de Cristo mountains, across the whole of Colorado, maybe on through Utah and Nevada? If they began to fall out, then he would continue the trail alone. He had sworn to get Gardner and nothing was going to stop him.

For a moment, a single instant, he felt inwardly shocked at the fierce depth of his anger. After all, Gardner was nothing more than another gun-happy killer who had dared to defy the law, no different from any of the others he had known. The evidence against him had been reasonably conclusive. Two men had identified him as the man who had gone into the bank, had come running out with a bag stuffed full of dollars, leaving behind him one of the clerks, lying bleeding to death on the floor.

He, Harbinger had not known the clerk who had died a few hours later, the fact that the bank had lost all of that money meant nothing to him at all. But a man was on the run from the law and it was his job to go out and get him. An eye for an eye and a tooth for a tooth. That was the only thing he lived by. Well, he told himself tiredly, a good night's sleep was what he needed more than anything else. Rob Gardner could wait for another few hours. So long as he knew which trail the other had taken, he could follow him clear to Utah. The thought brought a faint smile to his lips, drawing them back from his teeth and for a moment, his gaze rested on the gunbelt lying on the table, the light from the solitary lantern glimmering bluely from the metal of the butts. Maybe Gardner thought he was safe now. Enough money to get him some place where he could settle down and wait out a few years until everything had blown over and been forgotten. Some men had tried it in the past; and some of them had undoubtedly succeeded. But Gardner was not going to be one of the lucky ones. He stretched himself out on the bed, hands clasped behind his head, staring up at the low ceiling, listening to the faint noises outside in the street. A horse whickered softly in the distance. There was the brief tattoo of hoofs as a man rode out, heading north.

Harbinger felt himself nursing a very odd feeling and sleep did not come as he had hoped. This mood, this irritable and restless feeling, would not leave him; it had come on him during those moments inside the iron-caged cell as he had talked with Vereau, self-confessed bandit and the Lord only knew what else. He lay loose in his joints, with the cold smoothness of the bed under him, hard and solid. The solidness helped him a lot and he found himself thinking back to the days before he had taken on the work he now did, before the badge of United States marshal had been pinned on his chest. Those had been carefree times, full of the smell of a cool breeze coming down through the tall pines and blowing across his camp-fire out in a wilderness of stars and moonshine; or the vivid scarlet of a sunset on the buttes that lifted clear of the wide, stretching deserts. He tried to keep his mind there, but it was mere grasping at faint shadows which had no substance and there was nothing to hold on to. There was no way for him to go back to those times, not even if he threw up this job, tried to forget the past. There was a dull ache behind his eyes which indicated the intensity of his thinking. He had taken this job because it enabled him to kill and stay within the law.

A faint sense of shock went through him at that moment. It was the first time in more than fifteen years that he had faced this fact squarely, knowing it to be true. He had fenced around it, formed all sorts of excuses in his mind for accepting the Marshal's badge, but it all boiled down to this one basic fact when looked at quite objectively.

It was a queer thing to think about though. The law allowed him to kill these men he went after, paid him for doing it; and although there were those who maintained that some of the men he hunted were innocent, that had never stopped him in the past and he knew it never would. In spite of his earlier feelings, he now experienced a sense of grim amusement. His name was feared all the way along the frontier, ranked with those of the notorious outlaws, some of whom he had killed in the course of his duties as

Marshal. Every gunman knew that some time, somewhere along the trail, he would face a man either faster or truer with a gun than himself. Here, in the West, the law of survival was the first of all laws and ensured that whenever a man shot such renowned gunmen as Slim Benson, Ed Tyrone and Abe Harper, there was only one trail left open to him, one that led downward to his own extinction. Down into the same kind of grave as those men had gone into. The mere fact that he was on the side of the law would not alter that.

Lying there, he wished he had brought a bottle of whiskey into the room with him, to drown the sudden feeling of impatience that rode high in him.

2

The Wilderness

Rob Gardner crossed the brawling, swift-running river of a ford where the water ran less than two feet deep, yet even here the drag of the current caught at his mount's feet and threatened to pull it down, the smooth stones which formed the river's bed were an additional menace, but eventually, he reached the far bank, his mount clambering up the crumbling earth. He did not know these mountains yet he felt little unease. The first steely palings of an early dawn were just beginning to show far off in the east and the higher peaks were touched with a faint rosy flush.

The *arriero* trail started its gradual ascent into the red-firs which clustered the highland edges of the slopes and above them, stretching up into the still-dark heavens where a few of the brighter stars were still showing. The pinched-down mountains closed about him as he urged his tired horse along the upgrade trail. They sought buckruns and went angling along mountain slopes, over saw-toothed ridges and down into benighted caverns, still resisting the encroaching daylight.

He rode without hurrying, knowing that Harbinger and the posse were still many miles to the east of him, that even if they had made good time across the great desert of Colorado, they were still four or five days behind him. One man could always travel faster than a bunch of riders, but those days he had spent in Connaught had lessened his lead and he knew that once he cut through the pass here he would have to make better time if he was to stay ahead of Harbinger.

A little stray breeze ran through high branches as he rode beneath the tall firs. The ground underfoot was thick with the leaves and cones of many years and muffled the sound of his mount's hoofs. Slowly, the dawn brightened around him. He deliberately kept to the trail, watching for narrow tracks which occasionally led off through the trees, speculating idly on how many wanted men might be hiding out in these tall mountains, men on the run from the law, stepping off the trail and hoping that no one would take the trouble of looking for them. By the middle of the morning, with hunger gnawing at his stomach, he rode through an ascending canyon, came out above the treeline and saw, stretching in front of him, the shade and sunlight which lay on the endless, saw-toothed ridges and sky-climbing spires of stone, some far-distant, purpled by a faint haze, others so close that he felt the nearness of them as they crowded in on him from both sides. Lifting his gaze, he stared up towards the high, overhanging peaks and ridges. While he had been sheltered by the tightly-packed trees, he had had no impression of open spaces and distances; but now, out in the open for the first time since he had cut up from the trail far below, he was aware of the gigantic vista that lay spread out all around him. By degrees, the country roughened still further, the sunlight was reflected from the tall edges of stone glinting painfully into his eyes, glaring at him with sickening, dizzy waves that beat up from the ground underfoot and down on him from the ledges. He held to the crests of the ledges for as long as possible, passed through a small clump of stunted trees which afforded him no shade from the blistering rays of the sun, then moved on into an endless series of ravines.

They were long miles now. His horse was tiring rapidly after the long ride of the previous day and night. He had not stopped to make camp during the gradual ascent into the foothills, but had pushed on, hoping to make the pass before evening on the next day. Now, with the sun almost at its zenith, it was evident that he was not going to make it; he would be forced to rest up somewhere. The horse was both tired and doubtful as it picked its way cautiously over the needle-shaped rocks and around the huge boulders which lay in his path and it frequently stopped, to be urged on by a touch of the spurs on its flanks. In places, the trail dropped away on one side so steeply that it was almost precipitous and the horse's feet slid along treacherously in the loose rubble. The further they climbed, the worse became the terrain.

It was hard, difficult progress, monotonous and mean. The breeze had fallen now that he had climbed high and the dust kicked up by his mount hung in the air about him, getting into his nostrils, working its way between his clothing and his flesh until it felt as if he were being bitten by a thousand insects.

He rose with the switchback courses as the heat head increased in its piled-up intensity, higher and higher across the side of the mountains until at last he reached a short levelling off place where a wide creek, the torrent swollen by the melting snows, raced across his path. It had already cut its way deeper into the thin earth and what little vegetation had grown along its banks had been overrun by the water and carried swiftly down the mountainside. Beyond the creek, the ridges marched up towards the looming heights.

Riding to the water's edge, he paused to let his horse drink its fill, then forded the swift-running water. Once on the other bank, he reined up, slid from the saddle, took a quick scouting look about him and decided to make camp here. It seemed to be the most suitable place he had encountered since leaving the timber. There was a small clearing some twenty yards from the creek. He hobbled the horse, gathered a few handfuls of dry tinder which he found scattered among the rocks and built a fire. While he cooked some of his meagre stock of food, he smoked a cigarette, drawing smoke deep into his lungs, forcing his tense muscles to relax. The heat of midday was a heavy, burning pressure on his body and the heat from the punished rocks rolled back over him like a thick blanket, bringing all of the moisture in him to the surface, drawing it out through the pores of his skin.

He was a tall man, with a rangeman's looseness about his movements, a limber man with deep blue eyes, half hidden beneath the lazy droop of the lids. The deep tan on his face spoke of long days exposed to the strong sun, a man who lived by the horse and the rope. He ate slowly, drank the hot brown liquid that passed for coffee, then moved away from the dying embers of the fire into the shadow of one of the steep, upthrusting rocks beside the trail, dropped back on to his shoulders, pulled his hat down over his face, glad of the chance to rest for a while. There was no sound to break the great stillness except for the movement of his horse and the snapping crackle as the last of the faggots were burned up in the heart of the fire nearby.

When he woke, the sun was almost halfway down the sky, westering towards the high peaks. The shadows were long and black now across the trail and his mount stood with its head lowered. The fire had long since died completely and only a handful of grey ashes remained. He pushed himself up on to his elbows and turned over slightly on to his side. He sucked in his cheeks, rubbed the film of sweat from his face and tilted the hat on to the back of his head. There was a red mark where the sweatband had pressed into the flesh of his forehead.

How long had he been on the run now? It was getting more and more difficult to remember exactly. He had been moving fast to keep clear of the weight of fire that Harbinger could bring to bear against him if the marshal ever caught up with him. The longer he managed to stay ahead, the more men in the posse would drop out, he was sure of that. These men had no personal grudge against him.

Some of them might even have known the truth, that he was innocent of the charge of murder which Harbinger had brought against him, knowing that the papers which the marshal carried in his vest pocket, bearing Judge Kelvin's signature on the body were not worth the paper they had been written on. Everyone in Nebraska knew that Kelvin was an old man, that when he was befuddled with drink he would sign anything, particularly if it were presented to him by a man with Harbinger's reputation.

He turned over on to his back once more, reluctant to rise, wanting to pursue these thoughts to their logical conclusion. He knew that he could not possibly buck the whole of the outfit that Harbinger had at his back. All he wanted now was a straight chance at the marshal; but that was the way the other worked, if all of the stories that were told about him were true. He was a gunman, not a gunslinger, and there was a subtle difference. He preferred to wait until he could pick a time and place of his own choosing and that was invariably when his opponent did not have a gun anywhere near him and there was no chance of Harbinger being the one left lying in a dusty street with a bullet in him.

Bitterness came up into his mind, bringing with it a sullen anger that refused to leave him, but grew stronger every minute. Evidently Harbinger knew that he was innocent too, and therefore by what right did he hunt him down like this from one state to another? Hiding behind his badge, he claimed to every man that he was acting within the law, surrounded himself by a shell of righteousness that gave him the right to run a man down like an animal and shoot him in the back without any warning.

Rolling over, he got to his feet,

clamped the hat down more tightly on his head, walked over to the creek and stretched himself out full length on his stomach, drinking his fill of the ice-cold, clear water. Bringing his fists close together, ridden mercilessly by his feelings, he climbed on top of the flat rock that overhung the edge of the trail and stared down through the mists of the afternoon, back along the trail he had ridden through the night and morning. It was empty as far as he could see, all the way back across the stretching plain that lay due east of the range. Harbinger and his men would still be a long way behind, but even so, he did not doubt that they were still there, still on his trail. If the men of the posse fell out, Harbinger would ride on alone, a man who never gave up.

Swinging up into the saddle, he raked spurs along the animal's flanks, leaning low to ease the burden on the horse. The afternoon was well along by this time and there was an odd haziness to the atmosphere now, something he had not expected. Among these high ridges, he had thought that the air would be exceptionally clear, enabling him to see for miles in every direction, but the heavy, leaden humid air pressed against him with an almost physical force. It was not yet full summer and he knew only too well that storms could arise with a sudden unexpectedness in these mountains. During a springtime cloud-burst, the skies would open and send tons of rain deluging down, covering everything, flooding the creeks and rivers until they became virtually impassable. With this thought in his mind, he cast a swiftly apprehensive glance up at the sky overhead, and then at the towering peaks he still had to cross, before he could make his way down the far side, out into the arid, waterless wastes of the vast desert land of Colorado.

★   ★   ★

It was near six in the morning with a heavy stillness lying over the town when

Harbinger woke. There was a pale light filtering in through the window of his room and the air was still cold on his face as he swung his legs to the floor, stretched his arms over his head, then went over to the bureau and splashed icy water from the pitcher on to his face and neck. It shocked the life back into him and he dressed quickly, buckling the heavy gunbelt around his middle before going to the door of his room and stepping out into the silent corridor. He shook the possemen awake, ignored their curses at being disturbed at this early hour particularly after the late night and the long, hard ride the previous day. Still grumbling, the men ate their breakfast, served to them by a sleepy-eyed waiter who obviously thought nothing of having to get up from his warm bed to feed these men.

'Why all the hurry, Marshal?' asked Condon from one of the nearby tables. 'He lost five or six days when he put up in this place. We're gettin' closer to him all the time, but there ain't no sense rushin' into somethin'. I figure we'd best ride careful and keep our eyes open. Could be he's decided to lay an ambush somewhere along the trail. He could pick off a handful of us before we knew he was there.'

'You gettin' yeller?' muttered Harbinger ominously. He set down his empty cup with a deliberate slowness. 'If any of you want to drop out, then say so now. I don't want any man ridin' with me who's scared to back up my play when the showdown comes.' He turned his head slowly, staring at each of the men in turn, noticing with a faint sense of scorn how their eyes dropped away whenever they met his. A bunch of frightened men, he reflected grimly, ready to back down if only one of them would give a lead for the others to follow. Who was going to be the first to admit he was scared of meeting up with Gardner? he wondered.

None of them said anything, until Condon went on: 'I ain't yeller,

Marshal, and you know it. But there ain't no point in ridin' into an ambush and gettin' ourselves shot without warnin'. I'll meet any man in fair fight, but I don't relish the thought of bein' knocked off with a bullet in the back from some dry-gulcher.'

'He won't do that,' said Harbinger confidently. 'He's on the run and he knows how many of us are after him. A man hunted down by a posse doesn't waste time gettin' up an ambush, if he's got four days' lead on his pursuers. He rides hell for leather to try to lengthen that lead and that's just what Gardner is doin' right now, tryin' to get through that pass before we catch up with him; or before a storm swells the rivers so much he can't get through.'

Condon fell silent at that. Ten minutes later, they collected their mounts from the livery stable, climbed stiffly into the saddle and prepared to move out. There were few watchers. It was too early for the ordinary citizens of Connaught and the only movement came when a stocky figure stepped out on to the boardwalk fifty paces along the street, paused there for a moment and then stepped down into the street.

'You reckon you'll find this man you're lookin' for?' asked Crowder. His eyes rested on Harbinger's face. 'He could've headed in any direction.'

'I'll find him,' said Harbinger hoarsely. 'And when I do, I'll kill him and take his body back to Nebraska so that they can see there, that I always finish any job I have to do.'

'Does it mean all that much to you?'

For a moment, Harbinger said nothing in answer to that question, debating within himself what sort of answer he could give the other would understand. Then he said thinly: 'When I accepted this badge, I swore to uphold the law and bring in any transgressors. I've always done that. I always mean to do it. That's why I shall run Gardner to earth wherever he tries to hide, why he's as good as dead right now.'

Without another word, without a

backward glance at the silent figure of the sheriff, he jabbed spurs into his horse's flanks, sent it leaping forward along the quiet, dusty street. The rest of the posse fell in behind him in a tight bunch, their faces tight, their eyes bleak, as they followed him. Ahead of them lay a four-day ride before they reached the spot where Gardner was at that very moment, provided that they chose the right trail. But if there were any doubts on this point in Harbinger's mind, nothing of them showed through on his face, drawn together in tight lines around the corners of his mouth and eyes.

Soon, the town faded into the sun-hazed distance behind them as the fiery disc lifted from the eastern horizon and began its slow climb into the cloudless heavens.

Nightfall, and they checked their mounts on a rise of ground that overlooked the broad lands which led west to the Sangre de Cristo mountains. Tired men, they had had no rest during the whole of the long day, when minutes had stretched themselves out into individual eternities of blistering torture and saddle weariness, of tear-blinded vision, faces masked by the dust, lips and throats parched by the dry heat that shimmered around them. Nothing had relieved that terrible heat. The day was a punishment to the men and the dust which clung to the air got into their mouths and nostrils, even though they reversed their neckpieces and tied them over the lower halves of their faces.

Harbinger drove them on, giving them no chance to rest or slow their murderous pace. To every suggestion that if they did not slow their progress, they would drive their horses to the ground and finish the day on foot, he merely grunted, motioned them to keep up with him.

Now with night stretching in swiftly from the east, there was a little coolness in the air which fell like a balm on their scorched bodies. An hour before, the country had lifted from its monotonous flatness into rolling dunes and crevices of sand and coarse earthy gulches. Here and there, a lofty pine tree rose from the ground, an occasional advance sentinel, warning them that they were approaching the foothills. The hills themselves and backing them, the tall mountains, were there in front of them now, outlined against the last of the reds and crimsons which flamed the western heavens, marking the spot where the sun had gone down. Then the reds vanished and the world changed, became blue and purple and cool, filled with the aromatic smell of the distant hills, taking some of the day's sting from their limbs.

Harbinger lifted a hand and motioned Condon forward, waited with a faint show of impatience until the other rode up beside him. The Marshal pointed with a long arm. 'There's his trail,' he said tightly.

From where they sat, it was just possible to make out the narrow trail which branched from the main stage route, and led to the south-west. 'He's been travellin' fast,' went on the other. 'Little sign of his tracks here. We need to be certain that he went that way. We won't see much in the dark so we'll make camp here.'

Condon nodded, went back to the others and spread the word. Harbinger remained on the hilltop, staring out into the growing darkness. There was no water here, but they had crossed several swift-running streams during the day and their water bottles were all full to the brim. He was still sitting there when the fire was blazing behind him in a small hollow in the lee of the hill, thinking his own deep thoughts, his right hand lowered, the blunt fingers touching the smooth butt of the gun in its holster.

'You want somethin' to eat, Marshal?' called Sutton harshly. He turned from where he sat by the fire, the red glow flickering on his tight features, on the deep-set, sunken eyes.

Harbinger turned in the saddle without answer, walked his mount to where the others were tethered in a long line, fastened the reins around the riata which had been strung between two stunted trees, then came over to the fire, lowering himself heavily between two of the men, taking the plate which Sutton held out to him.

'If we find his sign, do we head up into those mountains?' asked Legrasse, short and thin-faced, lips twisted into a perpetual sneer.

'If he's gone that way — yes.' There was no emotion in Harbinger's tone. He did not bother to look up at the other as he spoke.

There was a long silence, built rather than broken by the snap and crackle of the wood on the fire. Then Legrasse said: 'That might be askin' for trouble. Maybe Gardner knows those mountains. But nobody here does. Pick the wrong trail there, get caught by a river in full flood and we could perish there.'

Harbinger thrust his lower lip forward and a peculiar hardness came to his face. Almost, it seemed as though he was poised there, ready to leap forward in sudden, unexpected action.

But his voice was soft and controlled as he said: 'We aren't turnin' back now for anythin'. He's only four days ahead of us now. Maybe he's realized the mistake of fallin' in with that outlaw back there in the jail in Connaught and when a man on the run knows that he's made a big mistake, he's liable to go on makin' them and that could be fatal for him.'

'You're only guessin' this,' said the other stubbornly. He seemed strangely bent on building a situation to force a point.

Harbinger bent his glance on the other, said sharply: 'Legrasse, I don't like your tone and what's more to the point, I don't like what you're tryin' to suggest either.'

The other made to rise, but sank back as the marshal rapped out harshly:

'Just stay where you are, Legrasse. You knew what was ahead of us when you rode out with the posse.'

'There was no talk of a ride lastin' twenty days or havin' to cross maybe four states, or even of goin' up into mountains like those yonder. And when we do climb 'em and make our way down to the other side, what do we find then? Those deserts that lie on the other side of the Sangre de Cristo range are the worst you'll find anywhere. The entire state is one huge dustbowl with very little water and the most difficult and treacherous terrain you'll ever find.'

'Gardner will have to cross it,' Harbinger said flatly. 'And we can carry more food and water than he can.'

'I still don't like it,' muttered the other. 'I've heard about the Badlands of Colorado. We don't stand a chance in hell of catchin' him now and you know it, although for some reason you don't mean to give up until we're all dead. Maybe your pride forces you to keep on ridin' after Gardner. But this thing means nothin' to me personally. I care little whether Gardner lives or dies.' He paused, then went on more meaningly: 'In fact, I ain't so sure now that he's guilty of these charges. Seems to me there could be — '

'Shut up, Legrasse!' Harbinger said sharply. His head went up and in the red firelight there seemed to be something almost diabolical about his face, with the lips drawn back to show his teeth in a bestial snarl of anger, his eyes narrowed to slits under the thick, black brows.

'And if I don't want to keep quiet?'

'Then by God, I'll kill you. Don't force me to, Legrasse. You're a good posseman but I must have obedience from every one of you. I gave you a chance to drop out in Connaught. Nobody took the opportunity.'

Tenseness came to the group of men seated around the fire. Legrasse stared up at the other, his face tight, his thoughts hidden at the back of his eyes. Harbinger's hands swung gently towards his guns, fingers spread stiffly.

'We'll finish this ride, Legrasse,' he went on ominously. 'Gardner is a criminal on the run, a killer. Whether you believe that or not, I *know* it.'

'How do you know?' The other's tone was flat. Condon eased his legs a little, moved back slightly from the fire. A few feet away, Sutton pulled a breath down into his lungs, moved out of the line of fire if there was to be any gunplay.

Harbinger's thin lips drew back into a tight, almost sneering smile. He had noticed these slight movements out of the corner of his vision, without once taking his eyes off Legrasse's face. 'You can't expect any of the others to back up your play, Legrasse,' he said solemnly. 'This is just between you and me. You've spoken out and it's up to you now. I don't want to have to kill you, but I will if I have to.'

Legrasse licked his dry lips, let his gaze slide nervously around the circle of men seated on the rim of the flickering fireglow, the red light playing over their faces. He saw nothing there to give him hope that any man would stand by him if he forced this argument to the point of a showdown. Slowly, his gaze moved back to Harbinger's remorseless glance.

'I don't figure you at all, Harbinger,' he said thinly. 'You got some personal grudge against this man?'

'He's set himself against the law. No man does that and gets away with it.' Harbinger leaned back and his hands were no longer quite so close to the polished butts of his guns. It was as if he had realized, at that very moment, that the other man had been beaten, that he did not intend to force a showdown. Legrasse lowered his gaze, stared down into the fire, shrugging his shoulders a little. The tension faded swiftly. Condon moved back to his place closer to the leaping flames as they carried red sparks high into the still night air.

The moon was a little past its meridian when Harbinger slipped under his blanket and stretched himself out on the cold, hard ground. The other men seemed to be asleep, but to be on the safe side, not trusting any of them now, he slid a Colt from its holster, and placed it inside the blanket where he could reach it in a single moment.

★　★　★

The main pass through the Sangre de Cristo mountains was a jagged scar of a trail that ran through miles of high peaks and lofty towers of stone, fluted and etched into weirdly fantastic shapes by long ages of wind and rain and snow. There was still snow on the higher levels, glistening in the pale light of dawn as Rob Gardner made his way slowly across a glittering creek, up through the sprawled, jumbled rocks which littered the trail at this point. The moon was well past its meridian, already beginning to pale a little in the steely dawn light and the air was bitterly cold, biting through his jacket, numbing his limbs and threatening to freeze the blood in his veins.

The night had been totally hushed for more than two hours except for the thin, high keening of the wind but now, without warning, there came a terrible, high-pitched scream that echoed from the rocks somewhere ahead and to his right. It was a sound that Gardner had heard only once before, but one which a man never forgot. The frightening cry of a cougar lived with a man all his life and he acted instinctively the moment it rang out in the deep stillness of the mountains. His mount came right up, snug on its bit and it took him several moments to calm the animal down. Gently, he eased the long-barrelled Winchester from its scabbard, checked that it was loaded, then held it tightly in his right hand as he searched about him with eyes and ears, striving to pick out the first sign of the position of the mountain lion. This was one creature he did not like having on his trail, knowing that it could leap out on him from a rock overhanging the trail and knock him from the saddle before he knew of its presence there.

He rode up a lifting stretch of the trail, straining his eyes as he let them roam over the jumbled boulders which formed the ground to his right. Topping the ridge, a blast of wind struck him forcibly in the face, coming up from the down-sloping canyon that lay beyond. He braced himself into this, squinted into the dimness, wished that he had waited until dawn before striking camp and moving off again. His eyes were nearly closed against the force of the wind, half-blinded by tears as he leaned forward in the saddle, head lowered a little.

Nothing grew here except for a few scattered clumps of nopal bush and cat-claw and in the pale light of the dawn the peaks of the mountain that loomed above him seemed blacker than before. He tightened his grip on the reins as his horse began to shy, guessed that the cougar was somewhere close although he could not see it. Drawing his brows together in a faint scowl, he turned a little in the saddle, threw a swiftly apprehensive glance behind him, half-expecting to see the slinking shape of the mountain lion moving along the trail at his back. But there was nothing there, no shadows that moved from one rock to another, bent on his destruction.

He let his pent-up breath go in a series of small pinches of sound through his nostrils, tried to suppress the shiver that ran up and down his sweat-bathed spine. Maybe it had moved off deeper into the rocks, not wishing to attack a man. Cougars seldom attacked men unless forced to do so by anyone driving them into a corner where they had no other choice, but from what he had heard, they were unpredictable creatures and could turn and attack without warning, leaping out of the darkness and —

His thoughts gelled swiftly in his head as the shadow moved at the very edge of his vision. Swinging sharply in the saddle, he brought up the rifle and managed to loose off a single shot as the cougar launched itself from the high rock. The horse shied away in the same instant with a frightened whinney and he knew with a sudden certainty that although the bullet had hit the animal, it had not been a fatal shot. There was no time for him to squeeze off a second shot. Almost two hundred pounds of solid flesh and muscle, claw and fang, hit him with an irresistible force. He was thrown savagely from the saddle with the beast on top of him, claws raking across his chest. His right arm was pinned under him by the sheer weight of the cougar. The animal's breath was pantingly close and offensive. The gleaming fangs reached for his throat as he struggled desperately to hold the creature off. Instinct made him forget the rifle, knowing that the weapon was worse than useless to him now. Releasing his hold on it, he exerted all of his strength, succeeded in getting his right arm free, knowing he had only one chance of staying alive. His numbed fingers curled around the haft of the knife in his belt, dragged it out. Pain lanced through his chest as wicked claws slashed at his tunic, ripping it to shreds, raking into his flesh. The pain jarred him to action. With a tremendous effort, he moved his right arm, plunged the long blade into the soft part of the animal's stomach. Blood gushed warmly on to his hand and dripped along his wrist as he withdrew the blade and thrust it in again with all of his fading strength. God, would the creature never die? Screaming savagely, the cougar threshed wildly now, still pinning him to the hard ground, still making it impossible for him to ride or even throw it off. But its struggles were growing progressively weaker as its life blood dripped from its wounds. Sucking air down into his tortured lungs, Gardner delivered the final blow, felt the keen blade of the knife slide between the cougar's ribs towards the heart. One titanic struggle, a moment's sheer savagery, and it was all over. He had scarcely enough strength left in him to heave the dead body of the creature off him and roll over on to his side. Pain burned across his chest and twisting his head, he looked down at the shredded cloth of his jacket, now red-stained, knowing that some of the blood belonged to the cougar and some was his own.

He lay there for several minutes, sucking air down into his lungs, fighting off the weakness and the sickness which threatened to overwhelm him. Weakly, he pushed himself up on to his elbows, stared about him in the steel-grey dimness. The cougar lay a few inches away, mouth hanging open, eyes glazing in death. At last, he struggled to his feet, stood swaying for a long moment, as the blood rushed pounding to his head, increasing the terrible, throbbing ache at the back of his temples. Clinging to the rocky wall of the canyon for support, he stood there, gradually getting some of the feeling back into his body. It was impossible to guess how much blood he had lost, but he knew that he would have to clean his wounds before infection or poison from the animal's claws got into his body.

Glancing about him through blurred vision, he saw his horse standing, trembling violently, fifty yards away at the far end of the canyon. Summoning up his remaining strength, he stumbled towards it over the rocky, uneven ground. Fortunately, it remained where it was, did not shy away from him. Had it done so, he felt certain he would never be able to catch it; and without it he would be trapped in these mountains, until he either died from starvation, or Harbinger and the posse came upon him. Either way, it would mean the end for him.

Somehow, he succeeded in pulling himself up into the saddle, thrusting the Winchester which he had retrieved, into

71

the scabbard. Tightening his grip with his legs around the horse's belly, holding fast to the reins, he urged it forward into the growing light of dawn, searching for a stream where he could make camp and bathe his wounds.

A retching spasm gripped him a few minutes later and had him jack-knifing violently in the saddle. He wasn't going to make it, he told himself fiercely, striving to hold on to his buckling consciousness. He glanced down at his shirt. There was fresh blood on the cotton and his initial hope that the deep scratches had stopped bleeding, faded at once. Perhaps, he reflected, the act of getting up into the saddle, had started them bleeding again, and the inevitable swaying motion was not going to help things at all.

The nearest creek should not be too far away now that he was heading down the far slope of the pass but the ride was beginning to tell on him though, in his condition. Sweat dripped from his forehead in spite of the chilling wind that blew along the canyon, ran down his neck and soaked into the collar of his shirt. His head was pounding incessantly with a thunderous roar and the tall rocky peaks seemed to be swaying and tilting all around him.

A second violent spasm seized him and then he was forcing the horse on at a faster pace, knowing it was his only chance. If he allowed it to walk slowly he could pass out from loss of blood long before they reached a stream. It was all he could do to remain in the saddle, clinging desperately to the reins in his efforts to hold on. He moaned aloud, digging in with toes, elbows, knees and fingers, feeling his flesh tearing with every movement, gritting his teeth to bite down on the agony that seared redly through his body, stabbing through his muscles and limbs. He was almost cashed in when they climbed a narrow rise, turned a sharply angled corner in the trail and came within sight of the creek which flooded down the mountain face. His hands were shaking violently now, his chest slippery with blood and sweat. He forced his sight through the curtain of tears and weakness, managed to rein up the horse on the edge of the creek and almost fell from the saddle.

Chest heaving, throat burning, the stuttering breath barking from him, he hit the ground hard, almost lost consciousness at that moment, but somehow succeeded in crawling over the hard, needle-tipped rocks until he reached the icy waters of the creek as they bubbled noisily over the smooth, flat stones where it had worn a channel through the rock.

Splashing the water on to his face and neck, he felt the shock revive him a little. Forcing himself into a sitting position, he pulled off his thick mackinaw jacket, then removed his shirt, ignoring the cold wind that swept around him, chilling him to the bone, congealing the sweat on his body. His flesh was criss-crossed by deep claw-marks which had ripped across his body during that death-struggle with the cougar. Gritting his teeth, clenching them tightly in his head, he soaked his neckpiece in the water and washed the blood and dirt from the wounds. The water stung painfully but it was a job which had to be done and he forced himself to go ahead with it until all of the grime and gore had been cleansed, washed away. Several of the deeper scratches still bled a little but this would wash them free of any lingering traces of poison from that animal's claws. Tearing a long strip of material from his shirt, he bound it tightly around his chest, then forced himself to his feet. But he was fortunate to be still alive.

The sunlight was washing in a great, moving wave over the topmost peaks, drifting down the fluted columns of stone although the pass itself was still in deep shadow. Lowering himself to his knees, he scooped up some of the water in a cupped hand and drank it down. It soothed the agony in his throat a little and he dragged himself over the wide trail, until he could sit with his back and shoulders against a high slab of rock, waiting for the sun to come up and bring a little warmth with it. Up here, among the high peaks of the mountain range, there would not be the same dusty heat that he had encountered down in the plains.

By the time the sunlight flooded into the canyon, weakness had come over him and his head drooped forward on to his chest, half asleep and half conscious. How long he remained like that it was impossible to tell, but the sun was nearing its zenith and he guessed he had slept for several hours. He felt stiff but the pain in his chest had subsided into a dull maddening ache and he was able to stand upright without the same faintness as before. He drained the water still in his canteen, then went over to the bubbling creek and refilled it.

Getting back into the saddle, he forded the creek, urged his mount up the further bank and began the downward ride which led into the vast, stretching desert lands of Western Colorado. Slowly, the temperature increased. Halfway through the long afternoon, he rode over the smooth rock floor of a large bowl, turned a corner and put the high peaks behind him. In front of him, the trail went down and down, winding and twisting in a series of curves until, far off in the sun-baked distance, perhaps three thousand feet below him, he could just make out where it meandered as a faint, pencil-like scar across the shifting yellow sand and narrow gorges.

He could not hope to get down there before nightfall. The land was deceptive here, growing rougher as he descended, always less inviting. There were patches of mesquite sprouting from the thin soil which covered some of the rocky ledges. Here and there were denser patches of scrub oak and halfway down the slope, he would have to ride through forests of thick timber. He swung north towards lower ground, seeking to cut through the timber at its narrowest point.

Behind him, he noticed the clouds which were beginning to gather over the high peaks, the way the sky was cut up by the dark streaks of cumulus, ominous and threatening. Shortly before the sun went down over the flat skyline far to the west, the first raindrops began to fall. A faint surge of anger worked its way through him. This was the last thing he needed, for the weather to turn against him.

He had hoped to make camp as soon as it got dark, but that was out of the question now. He had to keep on riding through the night. Maybe once he hit the plains, the going would be easier and he could find some place where he could rest up. Darkness fell; and still it rained. There was rain all through the night. It slipped in beneath the folds of his mackinaw jacket. It squeezed into his boots, it chilled him to the bone, yet still he rode, only half conscious, his dulled mind slipping occasionally into the black morass of coma. It was out of the question to hurry. His mount was as tired as he was, had to pick its way cautiously in the darkness. In places, the ground fell away on one side of the trail in a steep, dizzying drop, a vertical precipice which yawned beneath him. He thought vaguely of the reasons why he was running, told himself in his moments of rationality, that he ran only because he did not stand a chance against the band of men that Harbinger had with him. If the Marshal was alone, then he would turn and face him man to man, and only one of them would walk away from the encounter. But Harbinger did not fight that way. Gardner had heard talk of the killing Marshal's past reputation, had heard from men who had ridden with him, had been sickened by what they had witnessed. Shooting suspected law-breakers in the back from ambush, carrying their bodies back to the nearest jail and turning them over to the sheriff. How many men he had killed in that way, how many had been innocent of any charges which had been brought against them, as he was innocent, no one knew for sure. But there had been several of them, he knew that deep within himself. He was not the first innocent man to be hunted by Harbinger; and unless he could meet the other on even terms, he would certainly not be the last.

Still swaying in the saddle, he watched a grey reluctant dawn creep over the eastern lip of the earth. His thoughts went on ahead; he thought that there might just possibly be some small township down there before the stretching plains were reached. It was unlikely there would be one for several miles once he rode out into the far-reaching Badlands and his mind baulked at the idea of setting over that waterless, arid desert in his present condition. He felt a deep-seated worry too; at the thought of Harbinger, still on his trail, still somewhere behind him, maybe even starting the long drag up to the pass. That *hombre*, Vereau, who had kept one gun trained on him while forcing him to help in robbing the stage would have told Harbinger which trail he might take. Hope died a little more in his numbed mind as he continued to head down the slope.

3

The Haunt of Outcasts

Two days after Rob Gardner rode through the high pass and cut down towards the stretching plains which lay to the west of the Sangre de Cristo range, Jeb Harbinger led his men over a creek, so swollen by the heavy rains of the past three days that it was almost unfordable and up into the high foothills. There was no trail for them to follow. Any sign which Gardner might have left behind had been completely washed away by the torrential rain which had fallen on the mountains for almost two days without ceasing, turning the trail into a racing torrent which obliterated any tracks.

After reaching the other side of the creek, the party immediately pushed on towards the thick timber. They had spurred their mounts cruelly, mercilessly, during the ride across the open grassland but Harbinger had ignored all suggestions that they should rest up for a day, that Gardner would find it difficult to get over the pass even though he might find it still open.

Condon leaned low from his saddle as they rounded a sharp corner, pointed to a patch of grey-black which could just be faintly discerned against the rocks.

'Looks like somebody lit a fire here and not too long ago,' he remarked.

Harbinger gave a quick nod. 'Shows we're on the right trail,' he said thickly. 'Let's keep movin'.'

'How do you know it was Gardner who lit that fire?' Legrasse wanted to know. 'Could have been any trapper in these hills. The range must be infested with men runnin' from the law. There are a thousand places where a man can hide and it would take an eternity to find him.'

'It's his fire all right,' Harbinger

affirmed. He bent his hard gaze on the other. 'He's still goin' straight ahead for that pass that Vereau told me about.'

Legrasse shrugged. 'He might break off the trail anywhere along it. He stopped back there at Connaught, remember?'

'I haven't forgotten,' snapped the marshal. 'But break off where? There ain't no place he could break off here. He doesn't know the country and you couldn't possibly buck through this kind of country anywhere else. He has to keep on ridin' until he gets through that pass. Keep your eyes open for any further sign of his trail.'

He led them forward, eyes sweeping the trail from side to side. He was still unwilling to let go his hopes for an early capture; the desire drove him tautly and it was with ill-concealed impatience that he forced his mount to make its own pace while they looked to the ground along the sides of the trail for anywhere that Gardner might have turned off to make camp for the night.

There was nothing to be seen as they rode into the tall timber. The pine needles and fir cones had formed a deep carpet which would show no sign of a horse's prints. That evening, with the shoulders of the tall mountains pushing down on them from every side, cramping the twisting trail, they came to a narrow pass where the wind, funnelling down the peaks high against the sky, bore to them the faint smell of smoke and dark ashes.

Harbinger found the camp, spent precious minutes edging around it, then found that it had been abandoned even before the rains had come, swore softly under his breath, rode back to where the rest of the posse sat clustered on the trail. The men were muttering among themselves as he rode in out of the rocks, stopped as he appeared.

'He's been here,' he said harshly. 'We're not far behind him. That must be the pass yonder.' He pointed a blunt forefinger to where the rocky ledges dipped down a little nearly a thousand feet above them, the undulating skyline just visible against the sky-darkening heavens. 'We should reach it by tomorrow morning. After that, it's goin' to be easier. I figure we ought to catch up with him before another two or three days are past.'

Then, an hour later, with the starshine laying a shimmering glow over the smooth rocks, they reached the brawling river that plunged down the steep side of the mountains, cutting directly across the trail. Harbinger rode slowly forward to the bank, sat tall in the saddle, peering into the dimness. Beside him, Condon sucked in a sharp breath and shook his head in a meaningful gesture. The heavy rains and the melting snows had done their work well. The river was up and surging down the slope with a vengeance. White water spun in whirling eddies near the bank where the current had already gouged great lengths out of them, cutting them back by several yards, churning the earth into the middle of the streaming water, bubbling, frothing and thundering. Even as they watched, long trunks of trees came moving down, borne on the swift current, tumbling and leaping several feet into the air as they struck submerged rocks, twisting and crashing in a thunderous, boisterous confusion. Tall fountains of foam jetted high into the air, faintly seen in the dim starlight. It was a weird and strangely terrifying sight, a glimpse of nature in the raw.

'We're stopped right here until that goes down,' Condon said, and there was a deep and utter conviction in his measured tone. 'We don't stand a chance of getting across that.'

'We have got to cross it,' muttered Harbinger. His lips were drawn back over his teeth in a snarl of defiance. 'I'm not goin' to let a river stop me now that I'm so close.'

'You don't mean that.' Condon turned in the saddle, stared at the other in stunned surprise. 'It's sheer madness. No horse could swim that torrent.'

'Once they're put into it, they'll swim,' Harbinger said tightly. He hesitated for a moment, then deliberately put his horse to the water, to where the bank was literally crumbling away while they watched. The swirling water dragged at his mount's legs. Bubbles were churned up as it struggled forward, urged on by the other. It reached a spot where the sweeping, surging waters had gouged out a deep channel in the river bed. The horse swam, struggling to move against the current. Harbinger swore like a madman, pulled hard on the reins, urging the animal back towards the bank. Now he was almost twenty yards out, near where the water was more than thirty or forty feet deep and the horse, fighting the drag of the tremendous current swung in a wide semi-circle. Suddenly, the animal's feet struck a bar of firmer ground and it clambered up on to it, the water pouring off man and beast.

Condon swung his mount along the crumbling bank, spun his lariat expertly, dropped the line over Harbinger's saddle. His horse went back on to its haunches, taking the strain as the marshal grabbed the rope, made it fast on the saddlehorn and signalled to Condon that he was ready.

Kicking the mount's flanks, raking rowels along them, he forced the horse back into the surging, thunderous water that frothed and foamed all about him now. Huge logs, tossed like matchwood by the current, passed within a foot or so of the swimming horse, threatening to engulf them completely, to strike and carry them under, where the tumbling water swirled and twisted. Harbinger clung grimly to the taut rope as Condon edged his mount back, a foot at a time, drawing the other gradually closer to the bank. Five minutes passed; then ten. Inch by inch, the other swung through the teeming waters and at last he stood on firm ground once more, his dripping clothing clinging to his body, water streaming into his eyes, plastering his hair against his head.

Slowly, they made their way back to the others. Condon said shortly: 'You see how impossible it is to cross that river now. We'll have to wait a few days until it goes down.'

'We cross in the morning, at first light,' said Harbinger stubbornly. There was a hard glint in his deep-set eyes as he turned his head slowly, his gaze sweeping over each man in turn.

'No,' said Condon. He wiped the water from his face, brushing it out of his eyes. 'I'm goin' to rest up here until that flood settles. You almost died out there and — '

'I said we cross that river at first light,' Harbinger repeated ominously. 'Do we go on without you, Condon?'

'Yes,' said the other thinly. 'If you're determined to throw away your life like that, then it's your business. But I ain't losin' mine just for the sake of catchin' up with some *hombre* who's probably dead by now, gone over the edge of this trail way up near the peaks.'

Harbinger's scowl was a harsh

twisting of his mud-plastered features. 'Any other man think the same way?' he asked softly.

Benson, Hander, Cowdrey and five others stepped forward and moved up beside Condon. Their eyes were bleak as they faced the marshal. For a long moment he eyed them in tight-lipped silence. Then he said raspingly: 'Then God damn you all to Hell! We can continue this trail without you.' His fingers touched the butt of his gun ominously. 'You'd better ride now. I don't want to see any of you men again. Understand?'

'Don't worry,' muttered Cowdrey harshly. 'We're pullin' out right now. I never did like this idea of goin' across all this territory, huntin' down a man who might be innocent.'

'Damn your hide, Cowdrey. Get ridin',' roared Harbinger. 'I'll continue this hunt with the men I've got.'

Cowdrey said nothing, but turned his horse, rode off along the dim rutted trail which led back, down the mountain to the east. One by one, the other men followed him without a backward glance at those who remained with the Killer Marshal.

★   ★   ★

Coming out of the downswing, Gardner found himself moving through tall timber which grew along the lower slopes of the vast mountain range which he had just crossed. The dull ache in his chest still remained with him and the cold wind had brought a chilling numbness to his entire body. There was little feeling left in his fingers and he was finding it more and more difficult to keep a grip on the reins. Worse than the pain, worse than the crowding feeling of unconsciousness was the sense of being so utterly alone out here in this vast wilderness. Up above him were the looming peaks of the Sangre de Cristo mountains. In front of him were the great plains of Colorado. Where the nearest human habitation lay, he did not know.

The moon was just settling down behind the western bluffs, gleaming faintly on a wide river that ran alongside the trail a mile further on. Soon, the yellow scratch in the sky was gone as the moon set and there came the darkness before the dawn, the pale grey light having vanished half an hour earlier, the false dawn which one often saw in these parts.

Five minutes later, he came to the point where the trail ran on into the river. Normally, the water here would have been one or two feet, easily fordable. Now, with the current running strongly it was at least six feet deep in the middle. But there was no way around it. Sucking in a deep breath, he put his mount into the icy cold water. The shock as the current caught them hammered through his body. The bottom of the river dropped away suddenly and without warning his mount was forced to swim. Within seconds, it was obvious that he would have to swim himself, otherwise his tired mount would never make it against the tremendous surge of the current. Swinging himself weakly from the saddle, he gasped aloud as the water closed about him. Desperately he tried to keep his hold on the reins, to be pulled along by the horse as it struck out for the far bank but the weakness in his body was such that his hold was broken at almost the same instant that he hit the water. He went deep, came up to the surface kicking frantically, a wild horror in him as he tried to strike out alongside the threshing horse. He felt the sucking pull of the undertow that churned about him. He went under, then came up again, with the blood pounding in his ears, choking and gasping. He could swim but he had never been called upon to swim against such a current and in such a weakened condition. Blindly, he struggled on into the foam-splashed darkness.

He could see little in front of him, but he had marked the further bank and struck out feebly for it, but it seemed to elude him, to draw further from him no matter how hard he struggled to move in that direction. His clothes were a dragging leaden weight threatening to pull him down, his arms and legs felt wooden and useless. Once or twice, he allowed himself to go down in the hope that he would touch bottom, came up floundering wildly, finding there was no bottom.

When his knees struck a low bank of sand and gravel, he felt a distinct shock of surprise, fell forward on to his face in the churning water, clutched at an out-thrusting root and managed to haul himself feebly up the bank where he lay wet and panting, scarcely able to draw enough air into his lungs to supply his body with the oxygen it needed.

How long he lay there, sprawled, numb and chilled to the bone, unable to move a single muscle, with the water still rushing about past his ankles, seeking to drag him back into the current, he did not know; but gradually, he managed to find sufficient strength to haul himself further up the bank, then forced himself to his knees, looking about him, peering along the bank of the river, seeking any sign of his horse. Nothing there to meet the eye yet it must have reached this bank. Without his weight on its back, it would have had little difficulty getting to safety.

A growing sense of faintness and futility came upon him. Sand grated under his feet as he stood up, swaying a little. Staggering forward, he moved along the bank. Tall trees lined the water's edge and a handful of stars still showed overhead through gaps in the swaying branches, cold and remote, unutterably lonely.

He knew that both terror and fear could grow with this mood and fought against it, telling himself that he was safely across the river, that there was yet another obstacle between Harbinger and himself. He shivered convulsively. He could feel the stretching vastness of this country all around him, this great wilderness that was Colorado. Thinking back, he put his mind on Jeb Harbinger, seeking anger as an antidote to the fear and weakness; but still the fact that his horse seemed to have vanished into the darkness, increased his apprehension. The physical drain of the battle with the river, in his weakened condition, had left him trembling and when he first tried to walk along the narrow bank of the river he stumbled and almost fell, scarcely able to remain upright.

It was hard walking along the bank. Trees and upthrusting roots barred his way and bushes, thorn and mesquite formed vague, dark blurs in the dimness, unseen until he blundered into them. There were times when he was forced to move very close to the water's edge and he could feel the earth of the bank moving under his feet, sliding down into the relentless current. Now that the last of the moonlight had gone, he was forced to move through the darkness of the trees more slowly than if he had been out in the open. Some nocturnal bird hammered against a branch immediately over his head, sent a faint shiver through him as the sudden sound shattered the clinging stillness. He felt the cold needle-pricking of sweat upon his skin.

The pounding ache hit the back of his eyes and through his chest and he felt utterly spent, scarcely able to walk upright now, swaying from side to side, his arms hitting the trunks of the trees as he staggered around a wide, sweeping bend in the river. If he knew this country, he could have struck off through the trees, away from the river, but right now, he was forced to continue along the only landmark he had.

He sent his mind ranging for something definite to fasten on, to take his thoughts off his own weakness, off the chill numbness in his body and the terrible, beating pain. The walking had warmed him a little at first, but now a cold breeze, sweeping along the curve of the river, struck him forcibly. He had no destination really, only the faint, vague hope that he might sooner or later, come across his mount. If only he was walking in the direction and not moving away from where his horse had gone . . .

When the sun rose, he was still near the river, the trees still crowded down against the bank, holding tightly to the water's edge, and his strength was failing fast. Sunlight reached the countryside around him, filtering through the tall trees, sparkling on the rushing water, glowing on the dust in the distance, touching with red and scarlet the topmost peaks of the mountains. For a moment, he paused, drew himself up to his full height and cast a speculative glance at the towering peaks, the long sloping ridges and the deep clefts in high rocky places. His eyes were unfocused, wide-ranging and it was as if he could see beyond the huge boulders and jumbled rocks to where a grim-visaged man, driven by his iron determination and will, led a party of men on a trail of vengeance after him.

Queer how little Harbinger had crossed his mind during these past few days, but they had been so crammed with events that he'd had little time for wondering just where the other was. Reaching deep down into himself, he somehow found the strength to go on, but there was fresh blood on the strips of cloth tightly bound around his chest and he swayed as he moved, often having to grasp at a nearby tree for support as his legs threatened to give way under him. He pressed his lips back hard to hold down a groan as a stab of agony lanced through his body. He did not know how far he had travelled since he had swum the river but he seemed to have been stumbling on for an eternity. Both arms hung loose by his sides. He steadied himself, lifted his head with an effort, to push his sight through the curtain of red mist that hovered tantalizingly in front of his stultified vision. A dizziness swept through him and there was the feel of nausea in the bottom of his stomach, spreading swiftly into the rest of his body.

He couldn't go much further that was for sure. There was probably poison in his body, poison injected into his bloodstream by those raking claws which had torn his flesh almost to the bone. Sunlight glared into his eyes, cut redly into his brain, even through closed lids. Pausing, he bent and drank from the swift-running river. The water tasted of sand, grated on his teeth, but it cooled his parched throat and made him feel a little better.

A mile further on, the trail suddenly swung west, away from the river, through a long, steep-sided canyon, and then out into more open country, dotted here and there with thorn and mesquite; a wild, sun-glaring desert. With a tremendous effort, he stumbled along the canyon, paused when he reached the far end, his mind baulking at the vast distances which lay spread out in front of him. The distant horizon, shivering in the rising heat ahead, began to tilt and sway in front of his twisting vision. The blue-white mirror of the sky suddenly constricted into a huge fist that beat against his brain. It was as if someone had hit him on the back of the head with the butt of a revolver. Dropping forward on to his face, he lay still in the dust, arms outflung, his legs twisted beneath him.

★   ★   ★

Slowly, painfully, he fought his way back to consciousness. Several times he came up above the surface of reality, only to slip back again into the deep blackness, his mind lacking the ability to hang on to the brief, fleeting moments of rationality. Whenever he tried to open his eyes, he saw only darkness, deep and black and remote. He tried to lift his head, but a terrible throbbing ache forced him to lie absolutely still. Gradually, he became conscious of his limbs, knew that he was lying on his back on something softer than the sandy rocks in which he had fallen. His chest felt on fire and his arms and legs seemed swollen to twice their normal size.

What had happened to him? Where was he? How long had he been unconscious? A hundred urgent questions ran riot through his mind but he could find answers to none of them. He remembered that nightmare walk along the bank of the river, first in utter darkness and then in the faint light of dawn, moving through the trees and the rocky canyon with the sun lifting to its zenith and the waves of heat flooding down on him. But he could remember nothing after that. Gingerly, forcing down the nausea which threatened to overwhelm him, he pushed himself up on to his elbows, opened his eyes and peered about him. At first, he could see nothing. The darkness pressed down on him from all sides like a curtain of velvet, almost tangible. Then, slowly, as his eyes adjusted themselves to the gloom, he was able to make out the nearer objects. He was lying on a low iron bed and there was a chair close by and a square window in the wall which was not quite as black as its surroundings. Through it, he was just able to make out a few stars glittering against the night darkness and knew that he had been unconscious for at least twelve hours, possibly more.

Gritting his teeth, he felt the cloth around his chest. It had been replaced by something else and the warm stickiness of blood was absent. He lay back on the pillow with cold sweat breaking out on his forehead. Evidently he had been found lying there on the trail and had been brought back here. But where exactly was he and who was his unknown benefactor?

He lay quite still, sucking air into his lungs, staring up at the ceiling above him. The walls around him were made of logs and he knew he was in a cabin of some kind, probably one belonging to one of the trappers in the territory. Letting his breath sigh through his lips, he sank back weakly on to the bed and closed his eyes.

When he woke again, the stabbing agony in his chest was gone and he was able to open his eyes and keep them open. A pale grey light was filtering into the room and a moment later, the door opened and someone came in, closing the door quietly behind him. Gardner squinted round at the other as the man came over to the bed, stood beside it, looking down at him. The other was tall, bearded and with suspicious eyes but he grinned momentarily and said in a thick, hoarse voice: 'You seem to have had quite a fight, pilgrim.'

Gardner nodded his head feebly. 'You're right there, friend,' he acknowledged quietly. 'What happened? Did you find me out there on the edge of the desert?'

The other moved away and went over to the window, looking out into the greyness of dawn. 'You're a stranger in these parts,' he said soberly, not turning his head. 'Why are you here?'

'Just ridin' on through. Had a brush with a cougar up there near the pass. Managed to make it to the river, but lost my horse fording it. I was tryin' to find the critter when I must've passed out.'

'You on the run from the law?' It was a direct question, but there was little curiosity in it and nothing to indicate that the other's intention would be to keep him here until the law arrived and then hand him over. It was more than likely that this man was not on speaking terms with the law either.

'Could be. What's it to you?' With an effort, Rob tried to force himself upright in the bed, to swing his legs to the floor and rise to his feet, but a wave of weakness swept over him and he fell back feebly on to the bed.

'Better not try to move for a while.' The other had turned, now stood beside him. 'You've been unconscious for more'n a day. That wound was poisoned in case you didn't know it.'

'I guessed that might have been it,' Rob said, speaking through tightly-clenched teeth. 'Why did you bring me here?'

The other shrugged. 'Weren't no sense leavin' you out there, mister. You'd have been dead by now if I'd done that. Even if the heat or the poison in you hadn't finished you, the coyotes or a roamin' cougar would have done the job. Just why is the law on your trail?'

Rob grimaced. 'It's a long story and I'm not sure you'd believe it.'

'Try me,' said the other quietly. 'I got plenty of time and you won't be goin' any place for a couple more days anyway, not with that poison still racing through your veins.'

'I can't afford to lie up a couple of days,' Rob said harshly. He shook his head, swallowing to force down the sickness in him. 'That posse can't be more than three days away and once they cut through the pass, they'll make good time headin' down out of the mountains.'

The other shook his head emphatically. 'They won't get through the pass,' he said confidently.

'Why not?'

The man glanced down at him, grinning wolfishly, smiling thinly. 'No rush, mister. No rush at all. The rains have washed down a dirt slide which has blocked the trail the other side of the pass. Even if they get across the Beaver River which is real mean when it's in full flood, they can't get around that slide.'

'You sure of that?'

'I'm real sure,' acknowledged the other. 'They got to ride through that pass. Ain't no other way down this time of the year and the winter has been real bad. You've been hurt bad and you have to get some of your strength back before you can ride out of here. Once you leave here, there's nothing but two hundred miles or more of empty desert to cross before you get to Flatrock. And that's only the halfway stage. If you're bent on heading clear across Colorado, then you'll have another three or four hundred miles of canyon the likes of which you've never even dreamed of. It's the devil's country out yonder and there ain't many men who've tried to cross it and lived to get through into Nevada.'

Rob sighed faintly. Somehow, he believed what the other had said about the slide blocking the trail through the pass and it meant he had a brief respite. How long that blocked trail would hold up a man like Harbinger, he didn't know. Perhaps for a couple of days, while he found a trail around it. Knowing the Killer Marshal, he would not rest until he had worked his way around it, back on to the trail once more and if the rest of the posse refused to go with him, if they threw in their hands and turned back east, then Harbinger would go on alone. That was the sort of man he was. Once he got his teeth into something like this, there was nothing this side of hell that would shake him off.

'Goin' to tell me why you're on the run, mister?'

'Sure, if you want to hear it. I guess it all started in a place called Twin Creeks, back in Nebraska about a month ago. There was a bank hold up in town. Three men took part in the raid. As usual they all wore masks, one staying outside while the other two went in and held up the cashier and the customers who were in the bank at the time. They would've got away with it if one of the guards hadn't pressed the alarm bell and brought the sheriff and a handful of his men running. They got the two bandits who were inside the bank, shot them dead on the steps, but the third man shot his way clear of town, killed a guard in the process. They never caught him.'

'So?' The other lifted thick black brows in an interrogative glance. 'And where do you come into this deal? Why are they after you?'

'I was in town that day. I'd stopped on the edge of town to buy some stores and I'd just swung up into the saddle when this rider went by, ridin' hell for leather out of town. I couldn't see his face, but I guessed there was somethin' wrong and started out after him. I lost him a couple of miles out of Flatrock and it was then that the sheriff and his posse caught up with me. Before I knew what was happenin' they had their guns on me and I was under arrest, suspected of bein' the third outlaw. Nobody would listen when I tried to tell them what had really happened. The sheriff tossed me into jail and brought out a handful of men who were prepared to testify that I was the man they saw waitin' outside the bank, the man who shot dead the bank guard when he stepped out of the building. I tried to get the storekeeper I'd brought my vittles from to corroborate my statement but he'd somehow conveniently forgotten that anybody had been into his store around that time. I figure

111

the sheriff had probably paid him to keep his mouth shut so that they could tie up the case swift and simple.'

'So they framed you for the killin'?' muttered the other.

'That's right. I figured there would be no way out of it for me. Once they got the circuit judge into town and put me on trial everybody in Twin Creeks would've been convinced of my guilt and I'd have no defence at all. So I knocked one of the deputies over the head when he brought my supper and busted out of jail.'

The man gave a quick nod of understanding. Something seemed to be balanced in his mind but he said nothing for several moments. 'Funny they should follow you all the way from Nebraska and through Colorado. I'd have figured the sheriff's jurisdiction ended outside Twin Creeks.'

Rob's gaze was bleak. His brows pulled together in a faint scowl. 'That posse on my tail is led by Jeb Harbinger,' he said thinly. 'Now perhaps you can understand why I want to push on.'

'I've heard he's a killer,' muttered the other slowly. He raised a hand and scratched his cheek. ''Pears you're in bigger trouble than I thought. Still, they got no other way to get here and it's certain you ain't in a fit state to travel.' He moved towards the door. 'I'll rustle you up a bite to eat,' he said.

Rob lay on the bed, thinking things over in his mind. Glancing down at the rough bandages around his chest, he smelled a strange odour coming from them and for one wild, heart-thumping moment, as his nose wrinkled a little at the scent, he thought that the wounds had turned gangrenous, then he knew what it was. These mountain folk often had to doctor themselves or their own kind, used herbs which they gathered in the hills, brewing them all together into some strange witch's concoction which they used on wounds such as these. But they seemed to heal the torn flesh and draw the poisons out of the system.

When the other came back a little

while later, he brought a bowl of soup and some home-made bread which he set down in front of Rob. 'Reckon you'll feel like eatin' now,' he said gruffly. A lot of the hostility had gone from his eyes and voice. 'What's your name, young fella?'

'Rob Gardner.'

'Mine's Sam Freeman.' He rubbed his hawk-like, high-bridged nose with a horny forefinger. 'Bin livin' in these hills for nigh on thirty years.'

'You live here alone?' Rod asked in surprise.

'There's a handful of others close by,' murmured the other. 'We ain't a big community and we like to keep ourselves to ourselves, with no hindrance from outlaws or the law.'

Rob eyed him sharply. 'And when Marshal Harbinger comes ridin' through here as he's bound to do in a little while, what d'you intend to tell him — about me?'

The other grinned wolfishly. 'We ain't seen you,' he said dogmatically.

4

The Wide Canyons

Against the night's stillness and the foaming splinters of the stars, a tiny stray breeze ran across the tops of the trees, stirring the leaves and branches, bringing the smell of the river, of green growing things on its breath. The sap was rising in the trees, the grass was pushing through in fresh blades. Rob Gardner stood in the doorway of the cabin and peered into the deep gloom. A couple of horses were tethered to a rope stretched between two trees and they moved restlessly in the night.

Sam Freeman said quietly: 'I still reckon you're a fool, insistin' on movin' on at first light. You'll be safe here for another couple of days at least.'

Rob shook his head. His face felt tight and there was a coldness in his body which did not come from the night air, but something else deeper within him. 'You don't know Harbinger,' he muttered. 'He'll find some way of gettin' around that slide up there, even if he has to dig his way through it with his bare hands.'

Freeman shrugged. 'Those wounds o' yours ain't properly healed yet. And I sometimes wonder if you know what you're headin' into out yonder. It's bad country, scarcely any trails, no water and that blisterin' sun can turn a man mad within days.'

'Better to go out there than be caught by Harbinger.'

Freeman remained silent over a long period, bent forward a little in the doorway. He peered out into the darkness, oddly indrawn and sober. When he spoke again, there was a strange drag in his voice: 'You ain't the first man on the run who's gone through here, headin' out west, tryin' to stay one jump ahead of the law. Some were no better and no worse than average; a break one way had set 'em against the law and all they needed was a break the other way to set them back on the right trail again, if only they could ride on to some place where they were safe until the smell of gunsmoke wore off. More likely than not, their next break would be in the wrong direction, sending them further from the law. That's usually the way outlaws are made.'

'And you reckon I might go the same way?' Rob lifted his brows a little.

'Could be. I wouldn't like to see it. You've been accused of somethin' you didn't do and that can make a man real mean and bitter in his soul. He wants to fight the world his own way and if he's found it to be tough and evil, then he uses evil, tough ways.' He rubbed his cheek. 'The finest thing I know is to be able to ride into some strange town along the trail, sit in a canteen and have your back to the door and never have to worry about what's goin' on behind you.'

'I'll think that over,' Rob told him. He had discovered a strange liking for this man in spite of the other's gruff, suspicious nature. He was only one of perhaps a dozen such men, who had chosen to live out here in the wild; away from the rest of civilization, living off the land close to the earth.

It was a decrepit little community they had here but he reckoned they were as happy and content with their lot as most other men he had met along the trail, men who seemed to be forever searching for something at trail's end and never really finding it. It could be that these men had been more fortunate, that they had discovered what all the others were searching for.

The next morning, just as dawn was spreading a pale greyness over the high peaks to the east, limming them against the heavens, he saddled up one of the horses, tightened the cinch under the animal's belly. Freeman stood a couple of feet away, eyes lidded.

There was still a bandage around his

chest, hampering his movements a little but the stiffness in his joints was gone and the overall weakness had all but vanished. Gripping the saddlehorn, he swung himself up on to the horse's back. Freeman came forward, handed him up a spare canteen of water. 'I still reckon you're an all-fired fool ridin' out like this. Sure you won't change your mind and stay on for another day?'

'Thanks all the same, but I have to ride on now.' He glanced round to where the dawn was brightening swiftly. Sunlight would soon move over this land and presently heat would pour down on to the rocks. This place would get hotter than the hinges of hell once the sun lifted to its zenith and he had the sudden urge to be on his way, to put as much distance between Harbinger and himself as possible.

He rode out of the tiny settlement, out through a fringe of trees and came out into more open country. The pale light of dawn touched everything with a curiously eerie light and there was no sound around him apart from the steady abrasion of his horse's hooves on the hard, sunbaked earth.

An hour later, he rode out into the yellow sandy desert, the great wilderness of Western Colorado, away from the main trails, away from any water-holes, and the sand muffled the sound of his hard riding while the sun, a brazen disc in the cloudless heavens, lifted higher towards its zenith, the heat beating down on his head and shoulders, painful flashes of glaring light were reflected from the metal bits of his harness and bridle, into his eyes and he rode most of the time with his eyes three-quarter lidded in an attempt to shut out most of the vicious glare.

Freeman's words held their full meaning for him now that the wilderness was all about him. On his right, the long buttes stretched away into the desert, empty and shimmering in the heat haze. Overhead, he spotted a small flock of vultures as they wheeled in lazy circles against the brilliant, blue-white mirror of the sky. Here, in this vast, empty stillness a man could be lost for a score of years, with no one knowing what his fate had been until some prospector perhaps, stumbled on a pile of sun-bleached bones and paused for a moment to ponder the identity of the victim.

The sun reached its zenith and then began to descend slowly. The heat head reached its piled up intensity and he rode without pause, occasionally drinking from his water bottle to wash down the throat-clogging yellow dust which got into his mouth no matter how he tried to keep it out. His mount began to flag a little as he rode over the desert. He had been riding for close on six hours over some of the most terrible country in the entire territory.

A thin film of yellow dust lay on him now, dust which worked its way into the folds of his skin so that his whole body itched abominably. By the middle of the afternoon, with the dust devils chasing him, the conviction grew in his mind that this was going to be a day more terrible than any he had known on this long trail from Nebraska. He had known it was not going to be easy country to cross but now there was plenty of time for him to ponder the wisdom of riding out from that tiny trapper settlement when he had. Maybe Freeman had been right and one more day would have made no difference.

Far off on the horizon, a dark smudge behind the shimmering curtain of heat that lay over the desert, lay a range of low hills and now he allowed the stallion to pick its own pace, sitting tall and easy in the saddle. When a man had long distances to cover, he forced his mount on to a punishing pace at his own peril.

As he rode, head bent a little, he still saw everything there was to be seen. An old watercourse here, now dried up by the blistering beat of the sun, the winding shape of a vagrant trail in the sand, winding its way over a low ridge and vanishing in mystery over the other side. There was scarcely any movement around him. Only the occasional flash of purple as a sand lizard slithered from one rock to another, almost too quickly for the eye to follow.

The minutes stretched out, became hours. The sun dipped westward until it was shining directly into his eyes and all of the hardness, the cruelty of the ground was softened a little as the shadows began to lengthen, mottling the desert where it was slashed by the narrow ravines. Colorado was one vast desert once a man crossed the Sangre de Cristo mountains and if there was any really genuine softness in it then he had yet to find it. All about him there seemed to be a thousand miles of nothing but ochreous flats and the occasional rising buttes, fantastically etched rocks, red sandstone that lifted clear from the flatness, breaking the monotony but, if anything, serving only to heighten the feeling of emptiness and harshness which stretched from horizon to horizon.

He rubbed his forehead where the sweat trickled from beneath his hat, mingling with the sand and dust to form a thick mask on his face. All of this was wasteland waterless, sterile and covered with this alkaline, powdery dust that lifted from beneath the feet of his mount to chafe and burn. Somehow, he doubted if men would ever come here and try to make something out of this wasteland. The effort would be far greater than any worth that could be got from it. Making himself a smoke, he thrust the cigarette between his lips, struck a match with his finger and thumb and sucked back a lungful of the sweet smoke, letting it out slowly through pursed lips. All of these days on the trail, with Harbinger and that posse continually on his back, had wearied him to the bone.

Even if he had not been scratched and almost killed by that mountain lion, the weariness would still have been there. When a man is on the run, he always loses a little weight, his cheeks sink down on to the bones and he has a haunted look about him. It had been relatively simple for Sam Freeman to have guessed that there were men after him somewhere along the trail, hounding him, giving him no rest at night. It was a look which few men could hide successfully.

At sunset, his horse slowed its pace of its own accord. Rob could feel the weariness in it, knew there was no sense in trying to urge it on at any faster pace. Another mile and he was very close to the low hills which he had noticed on the horizon before midday. They stretched for perhaps ten miles along the edge of the trail where it wound around them before heading out over the flats again, out towards another limitless horizon.

Here and there, stood a lonely pine, a forerunner of the scattered timber which grew dark on the low folds of the hills. Black and bulky, the smooth-topped crests stood out starkly against the vivid crimson of the sunset. The sun had vanished behind the hills, had gone down in a burst and a splash of flame and the few clouds in the west took on the colour, held it for a few moments and then let it go as the blue-purple of the night came swiftly in from the east to swamp the fiery sunset.

Rob drew himself tall in the saddle as coolness flowed against him, the faint breeze sweeping down from the low hills, touching his sun-scorched face, taking the sting of the heat out of it. He removed his hat, ran his fingers through his hair where it was plastered down against his scalp. The sweatband had made a red, painful mark across his forehead and he rubbed it gingerly with his sleeve.

The smell of the world was suddenly a different smell to that which had assailed his nostrils throughout the whole of that long day. He smelled sage and the aromatic scent of pine needles, moved almost unconsciously off the trail and into the hills, made his camp in a small clearing at the foot of the tall, sky-rearing pines. There was no fear of men coming on him without warning and he went into the undergrowth for dry tinder and faggots, gathering up more than he really needed, building a fire of his own. He sat and smoked a cigarette in the brilliance of the leaping flames as they crackled along the resinous twigs, the glow reflected redly from his face, his food cooking over the fire.

Through gaps in the branches overhead he could see the brilliant stars, so close it was as if he had only to reach up to be able to touch them with his outstretched fingers. He ate his food slowly, washing it down with cold water from his canteen. Then he unwrapped his bedroll from the saddle, hobbled his mount and took the blankets a few feet beyond the ring of firelight in the clearing, spreading them out on a soft matting of pine needles and tough moss.

★   ★   ★

East of the wide desertlands — as yet beyond the small settlement of the trappers — but swinging down from the peaks Jeb Harbinger led the posse through the wide pass, cursing the earthslide which had blocked the trail and held them up for almost two days before they had eventually succeeded in digging a way around it. Mile on mile, they had ridden along a stony, twisting trail with a yawning precipice on one hand and the sheer rock wall of the mountainside on the other, before they had reached the pass, found it still open, and ridden on through. Now, with the sun dipping towards the west, flooding the wide plain far below them with an eerie red light, they rode hard, but watchful, following the faint trail which was still visible to a keen eye.

'It's not easy to follow his sign now,' grunted Adams, riding beside the tall, bull-shouldered figure of the marshal, leaning forward a little in his saddle. 'Rain's washed a lot of it away.'

Harbinger glared at him in the fading

light. 'Ain't no other way he could have gone,' he said sarcastically. 'We'll pick up his trail better once we get out of these godforsaken mountains. Rock doesn't hold footprints long. But there will be soft earth down there and I'm figurin' that most of the rain in that storm fell here in the mountains.'

'There's a small settlement down there just beyond the river,' muttered Adams. 'Think he could have headed there?'

'If he did, and he reckons he can stick around, he's mistaken,' muttered the other grimly. He touched the butt of his Colt absently. 'We'll smoke him out and kill him.'

'Don't you figure he's entitled to a trial?' asked Morando, riding a little way behind the two men. 'So far as I heard, he ain't had no trial yet.'

'That's right.' Harbinger snapped his head round, stared at the other out of slitted eyes. 'He's foregone that right. Don't forget he busted out of jail and if that ain't the stamp of a guilty man, then I've yet to see it. Don't try to find excuses for this killer. There's a bank guard lyin' in Boot Hill back at Twin Creeks, with Gardner's bullet in him. Save your pity for him, not for this gunhawk we're huntin'.'

'I still say he's got the right to be tried with judge and jury,' said the other stubbornly. 'If he's guilty, then he'll hang. But at least, we'll know we don't have an innocent man's blood on our conscience.'

'So it's your conscience that's worryin' you,' grated Harbinger thinly. 'I say we finish him as soon as we catch up with him. If you think I'm riding more'n a thousand miles just to take him back alive, havin' to watch him every inch of the way in case he tries to make another break for it, you're mistaken. I'm in charge here and I say that he dies.'

Adams interrupted quickly: 'Somethin' yonder, Marshal. Just on the edge of the trail.' He pointed to the dark shadow that lay near the rocks.

Harbinger reined his mount sharply, slid from the saddle on the run, and went forward, bending beside the body of the cougar which lay huddled close to the boulders which formed the rocky wall along this part of the trail. He examined the body carefully, then straightened up, nodding slowly to himself as though satisfied by what he had seen. 'Stab wounds,' he said tersely. 'Could have been made by a Bowie knife.'

'Gardner?' Morendo looked down impassively.

'I reckon so. This cat's been dead about three days, I figure. Only Gardner could have done it.' He struck a match and bent down again, peering closely at the dead animal. Then he called: 'Adams. Take a look at this.'

Adams slid from the saddle, went forward and bent on one knee close to the other. Harbinger pointed towards the half-sheathed claws of the big cat.

'Blood,' said Adams after a brief pause. 'Looks to me as though Gardner could be hurt bad.'

'It looks that way,' agreed the other. He stood up. 'I've known some men who got into a fight with one of these cats. Even if they managed to kill the brute, they often died of poisoning. We'd better keep our eyes open from now on. It could be that Gardner didn't make it to that settlement.'

They stepped up into the saddle again and Harbinger motioned the men forward with a wave of a huge arm. After that, they rode in silence, eyes alert, watching the trail for shadows. Darkness came down and still they rode through the great rocks and around the deep chasms that opened in front of them without warning. It was a dangerous trail in the night but not once did Harbinger show any sign of altering their pace. Off to the right, intermittently visible, was a vast, sheer-rising peak which dominated the dark skyline in that direction. To their left, the rocky ledges lay closer, pressed down on them in tall shoulders of obsidian outgrowth. Holding to the trail was no easy matter. There were fresh slides of earth every few hundred yards where the heavy rain had washed down any loose soil on to the trail. But they did not encounter a massive slide such as that which had held them up for three days or so on the other side of the pass, but they lost time working their way around these obstructions, edging their frightened, panicky mounts an inch at a time with scarcely two feet between them and the steep drop on their right.

Sometime during the early hours of the morning, they halted in the first growth of pine on the lower slopes. The moon, half full had just risen and its pale yellow light showed them the dark shadow of the trees sprawling in front of them, a dark-green mass in the moonlight.

'We'll rest up here for a couple of hours,' Harbinger called. 'And remember that Gardner may be just out there with that Winchester of his, ready to pick off anyone who shows himself.'

Adams glanced cautiously into the thick, tangled underbrush which lay all about them before sliding down from the saddle. He pulled out his tobacco pouch, rolled a cigarette with fingers that shook a little. The other possemen were uneasy too.

Morando moved over to where Harbinger stood on the edge of the trees, where a steep rocky ledge sloped down towards the distant rocks far below them. He felt bone tired but tried not to show it. There had been many moments on the trail when he had asked himself why he had agreed to ride out with Harbinger in the first place. Certainly he had never expected the trail would lead them as far as this, across one state and maybe across another before they finally caught up with this *hombre*. He wondered whether Condon had been right about Gardner. He himself had not considered the other's innocence or guilt during the whole time they had been trailing him. Yet there must have been something to point to Gardner's guilt otherwise, he told himself fiercely, Harbinger would not have gone to all of this trouble, this discomfort, just to run him down. It would have been different if there was a personal score to settle here; but he knew of nothing like that.

He glanced sideways at the other, noticing the hard profile faintly illumined by the moonlight which slanted through the branches of the trees, touching the hawk-like nose, the flared nostrils as the other drew a deep breath into his lungs, the narrowed eyes which were never still, always watching the trail, looking ahead through the shimmering heat haze or into the cold, biting wind of the mountains, as if he could pick out the tiny shape of the man he hunted somewhere far in the distance.

And this man Gardner. Morando had never met him, would not even recognize him if he saw him face to face, and yet he was riding along with Harbinger to kill him. This was nothing new to the Killer Marshal. Jeb Harbinger had ridden out and hunted down more than a score of men, if the tally was anywhere near the truth. All of them he had brought in dead. Some said that most of them had been shot in the back, clearly from ambush, but he did not know how true that was. Could be it was merely a tale spread about by men envious of the other's reputation.

He sucked in his cheeks, pushed the thought of what lay in Harbinger's past out of his mind. All that concerned him now was what was likely to happen in the future. Would Gardner stand and fight when they finally ran him to earth? Or would he try to keep one jump ahead of them until they cornered him like a rat and destroyed him? It was something he could not answer without knowing more about the man they were hunting.

'You got somethin' on your mind, Morando?' asked Harbinger suddenly.

The other glanced round sharply, caught the marshal's heavy glance on him. 'Just wonderin' to myself what sort of man this Rob Gardner is,' he said in a low tone. 'Seems to me that if we're ridin' out to kill him, we ought to know what sort of *hombre* he is.'

'He's a cold-blooded killer. That's all you need to know about him,' said the other harshly.

'I don't figure it that way. I ain't denyin' that I've killed men in my time, but I've always had a damned good reason and I've known the sort of men they were before I had it out with them.'

Harbinger grinned mirthlessly, lips drawn back over his teeth. He moved his gunbelt slightly with his fingers hooked into the heavy leather. 'Most of the men I've hunted, I've known only from their pictures on a Wanted poster. There weren't nothin' personal in it at all. It made no difference to me what sort of men they were. The law wanted them, dead or alive.'

'But why bring 'em all in dead?' Morando wanted to know.

'Saves the county expense of a trial, of getting the judge out to the county town, and there ain't no chance of him escapin' or of any friends he might have bustin' him out of jail.'

Morando nodded. He had the inescapable feeling that there was more to it than that, but he said nothing, merely turning over what the other said in his mind.

'That settlement at the bottom of the hill trail,' Harbinger said after a long pause. 'You know anythin' about it?'

'Not much,' confessed the other. 'Just a handful of trappers here the last time I came through, maybe two, three years back.'

'You reckon they might hide Gardner, especially if he was hurt bad by that big cat?'

Morando mused on that for a moment, then shrugged. 'Could be. These mountain folk are real unpredictable. They might shoot you down the minute you rode into their village, or they might treat you royally. Depends a lot on what they think of you. If you mean would they turn him over to us just because we represent the law, then the answer is — no. They ain't got much respect for the law. They come out here to get away from things like that. They have a code all their own and they live strictly by it.'

'So it's unlikely that we'll get any help from them.' There was an ominous quality to the other's voice and his features bore a tight expression as if he were thinking of a great many things and not liking any of them.

'I guess you'd better expect no help from any of them,' Morando said quietly, decisively.

'And if I insist that they tell me anythin' I want to know?' The ruthless quality was quite evident now in his voice.

Morando stared at him for a moment before saying: 'Somehow, Marshal, I don't think that would be wise. I know we represent the law, even here in Colorado, but these men could part your hair with a rifle at three hundred yards and if you was to put their hackles up, they might just do that, without us even knowing they were there.'

Harbinger lit a cigar and drew on it thoughtfully, staring down at the redly glowing tip in the dimness. 'How many of them are there, did you say?'

'Hard to tell now. About a score when I was here last, but times may have changed. The place may have been abandoned by now, though I doubt that.'

'We'll head there anyway,' nodded the other. 'It's a safe bet that Gardner will have done so if he's as badly hurt as we think.'

They rested the horses and two hours later, rode out, through the trees and then along the twisting downgrade trail. Through scattered pine stands they moved down the mountainside, entered a draw that was narrow and almost completely overgrown with brush, so that they were forced to ride in single file, feeling the gradual descent and when it finally opened up they were almost in the foothills, riding towards the brawling river which thundered across the trail.

'We'll wait for first light,' Harbinger said, 'and then cross. There's a strong current here and he may not have been fool enough to put his mount in, knowing that his condition was such that he might never reach the other side.'

'Ain't no place for him to go if he stayed this side of the river,' said Morando. 'It just curves back on itself, forms a trap against those outjutting rocks yonder about half a mile away and if he went that way, he'd have to head back up into the mountains once more.'

Harbinger rubbed his brow. 'It ain't likely he'd do that,' he acceded. 'But I want two men to check along the bank. See if you can pick up his trail on this side. I'll feel a little better in my mind if I know that he went across.'

The two men he motioned to broke

away from the group and headed in different directions, keeping close to the water's edge, but wary of the still crumbling bank, bending low in the saddle as they scanned the soft ground for any prints which would indicate that their quarry had kept to the eastern bank of the river.

'Could be he tried to cross and got swept away,' said Adams tightly. He jerked an arm in the direction of the jetting plumes of white foam which were thrown up from the middle of the river where the current cascaded on to the half-submerged rocks. 'That cat gave him a bad mauling before he managed to finish it off. He must've lost quite a lot of blood and if he slipped from the saddle, he wouldn't have the strength to swim to the other side against that.'

'We'll soon know, if the others find nothing here and we can't pick up a trail anywhere on the other side.'

The first scout came back twenty minutes later, followed shortly by the second. Both reported that there was no sign that Gardner had remained on that side of the river, that he must have gone across, injured or not. Harbinger merely shrugged non-committally at the news, almost as if he had been expecting it. 'All right,' he said finally. He glanced up at the sky, at the moon now lowering towards the west and the stars paling in the east where the first flush of dawn was just beginning to show.

With the first steel-grey light, they urged their tired mounts into the racing, burning water, fought the drag of the strong current. Once they reached the deep part of the river, the men were forced to slide out of their saddles and tread water, keeping a tight hold on their reins, allowing their mounts to pull them through the foaming water. The horses responded gallantly, breasting the water so that it creamed off them, struggling towards the far bank, inch by inch. White water in the deep narrows, a brown flood of muddy, sandy water in the middle. The horses were drifting downstream at an alarming rate, but somehow they succeeded in reaching the other bank. It already lacked less than an hour to dawn and the chill cold closed about Morando like a blanket and he fought the harsh chill in his legs where the water had soaked him to the skin. Harbinger turned, sat tall in the saddle and studied the ground on this bank.

'If he crossed the river at all, he'd have come ashore somewhere close by,' he said. 'Look for any sign.'

They found it ten minutes later and Harbinger stared down at it with a puzzled scowl drawing the thick brows together into a hard line. 'He went along the bank on foot,' he said eventually. 'That don't make sense. What happened to his mount?'

'Could be the cougar killed it,' suggested Morando.

'Or he lost it in the river,' put in Adams tautly. 'That's more likely to be the answer. He wouldn't have attempted to swim the river in the first place if he had no mount. He'd have been forced to stay on the other bank.'

'I agree with that,' muttered Harbinger heavily. 'Let's move along. Without a horse, and injured by that big cat, he can't be too far ahead.'

Morando said sharply. 'He's probably lyin' in wait for us somewhere in the trees, maybe hopin' to take a couple of us with him before we kill him.'

'Then keep your eyes open and your head down,' snapped the marshal.

In single file, they moved along the narrow bank of the river, heads low to avoid the overhanging branches. In places, Gardner's trail was easy to follow. The muddy banks had held his footprints well, but where he had blundered off the trail into the tangled underbrush, they lost them for a while, edging their mounts slowly forward until they picked them up once more. Harbinger's eyes were narrowed speculatively.

He pointed to a low branch which

thrust itself from the brush. There was a small strip of something white hanging from it. Reaching out from the saddle, Morando grabbed it, eyed it curiously for a moment and then handed it to the marshal.

'Guess we've been on the right trail all along,' said Harbinger, with a note of triumph in his voice. 'There's blood on this. He must've used it as a bandage.'

No more was said as they rode out with Harbinger in the lead, and Morando and Adams following close behind. The country through which they rode was new to Harbinger. When they came to the point where Gardner had left the trail and plunged through the trees, heading away from the river, he would have ridden past it if it had not been for Morando. The half-breed's eagle eyes spotted the snapped twigs and crushed fern which showed where a man's body had crushed through them. They followed out the twisting, intersecting depths of the hushed forest, clattered over dry-washes, cut along the forested maze that had Harbinger completely lost and with the sun just beginning to lift over the far horizon of the desert which stretched away in front of them, came out of the long out-thrusts to the west.

Harbinger, looking massive with the high collar of his thick coat turned up against the biting wind, concentrated on the ground ahead of him as he casually reined his horse along. There was a noticeable lessening of the chill now that they came out into the open and Harbinger noticed something else. The wind was perceptibly fading, the gusty, turbulence smoothing into an even breeze.

Riding carefully down a treacherous shale slope, they reached the bottom just as the sun came up with a mighty bound and the air cleared suddenly. Morando produced a plug of tobacco, bit off a wad with a wrench of his neck muscles, soberly offered it around and got only negative headshakes, worried off another corner of it and pocketed the rest of it.

'There,' said Adams tightly. He pointed.

Harbinger was out of the saddle in an instant, kneeling on the flinty ground. His face was grim when he looked up. 'He was here all right. Probably passed out. There's blood on the ground. But somebody came along and found him here, carried him away.' He thrust his lower lip out in a scowling grimace, looked up at Morando. 'Seems you were right about these mountain trappers. They are the only ones who could have found him and taken him away. You know where these folk live?'

Morando nodded. 'You goin' to tangle with them, Marshal?'

'If I have to — yes. If they still have him there and hand him over to us real peaceable, then there'll be no trouble.'

'They won't hand him over,' said the half-breed with conviction.

'Then we shall have to take him by force,' was the tight reply. Climbing into the saddle, he motioned Morando to take the lead. 'I don't intend to let anybody stand in my way.'

Crossing a bare bench, they reached more timber. Half an hour onward they came upon a canyon at the bottom of which, a creek ran white and swift, bubbling in shadow. Somewhere nearby, but out of sight among the trees, there was the rumbling thunder of a falls, making a steady abrasive racket in the dawn stillness and the faint, eddying mist of its spray reached out of the damp undergrowth and closed about them as they rode alongside the canyon, the chill fog lying on the unmoving air. The road led them on through a clearing, past a broken-down shack which had obviously lain deserted for many years and then into a wider clearing. Around this opening in the trees, were almost a dozen cabins, some mere lean-to's thrown up out of logs. A dog came out of the shadowed interior of one of the cabins as they

149

rode up, a mangy, half-starved creature with its ribs outlined under the skin. It bared its teeth, revealing the red of its mouth.

Harbinger's hand reached down and closed over the butt of one of the Colts in his belt, then eased off as a voice muttered something from inside the hut. A moment later, a man stepped out into the open. There was a rifle held loosely in one hand and a long-bladed knife thrust into his belt. Hard-faced, with a black beard and eyes that stared piercingly at them, he was about six feet in height, thin, with little more than bone and hide on his lanky frame. It was impossible to tell how old he was. His features were indefinable, could have been those of a young or an old man. When he spoke, his voice had a faint edge to it, a sharp way of speaking the syllables.

'What do you want here at this time o' the mornin'?'

'We're law officers,' Harbinger said tersely. 'We're trailin' a man who's wanted for murder back in Nebraska.'

'You're a little outa your way, aren't you,' said the other with a trace of insolence. 'This ain't Nebraska. This is Colorado and we don't have the same law as you do back east.'

'Maybe not,' said Harbinger, keeping his tone even, in spite of the tight anger which seethed within him. Evidently Morando had been right about these folk too. They were not going to be co-operative with the law, probably had Gardner tucked away somewhere in one of these shacks at that very moment. He let his glance drift away from the man standing in front of him, eyeing the half-open doors of the other shacks around the perimeter of the clearing. He thought he saw movement in most of them but it was so dark in their shadowed interiors that he could not be sure. That little spot between his shoulder blades was itching though, the feel of eyes on his back and of unfriendly fingers on the triggers of rifles covering them from every direction.

'Then why come here?' persisted the trapper.

'This mean anythin' to you?' Harbinger flipped back his jacket, revealing the Marshal's badge. 'My name's Harbinger — Jeb Harbinger. I'm a United States marshal and I got a warrant for a man called Rob Gardner. We followed him over the Sangre de Cristo mountains and we know he had a tussle with a cougar up there, that he got himself hurt pretty bad. His trail leads down here and I'm figurin' that in his condition he'd never have been able to go more 'n a few miles from the river back there without passin' out.'

'So?' The other's gaze was disconcertingly direct.

'So I guess he must've been found by one of you and brought here.'

The trapper stolidly accepted that piece of information, chewing it over in his mind. He shrugged his stooping shoulders and his lids crept closer together, accentuating the beady expression in his eyes. He laid a glance on Harbinger that was like the edge of a knife, sharp and ready to cut.

'What you goin' to do with him when you do catch up with him?'

'Shoot him,' said Harbinger tightly, swiftly.

'Don't he get a trial — or anythin' like that?'

'He bust out of jail and rode on over the hill,' Harbinger said. 'To my mind, that means he's as guilty as hell. He don't rate a trial.'

'Guess that's your business,' grunted the other. He half turned to go back into the hut, then stopped as the marshal's voice rang out harshly: 'I know he came here and if he's hurt as bad as I think he is, then he'll still be here. If you're hidin' him, then you'd better turn him over to me pronto, unless you want me to go through every shack in this community, lookin' for him.'

'He ain't here,' said the old man

153

stubbornly. His grip on the rifle tightened perceptibly and he lifted it a little, holding it now in the crook of his arm, facing Harbinger directly.

'I don't believe that.' Harbinger nodded towards a small group of men who had come out into the clearing, were watching them sullenly. 'Somebody from this place found Gardner lying unconscious back there on the trail and brought him here. I want to know who it was and where you've got him hidden. If you don't tell me, then I figure I'll have to string one of you up, just to show the others that I mean everythin' I say.'

'You ain't stringin' up nobody,' said the trapper. He made to swing the rifle, then stopped as Morando, seated in the saddle a little to one side said: 'Drop that rifle, old-timer or I'll drop you.'

'You got no right to come here and — '

'I'm the law,' said Harbinger. 'And I say that you're actin' against the law if you try to hide a wanted murderer, and

154

refuse to co-operate with me. Now drop that rifle and quit stallin'.'

For a long moment there was no move on the trapper's part to let fall the rifle. His glance flickered to the other men standing in a small knot fifty yards away.

'Mister,' said Morando, his voice going softly quiet amid the trees so that it carried no further than the man in front of him. 'Mister, if they make any funny moves, you're a dead man. Now, for the last time, let go that rifle — or use it.'

Tension crackled in the clearing. Anything could have started the guns talking if it were to continue for another sixty seconds. But at last, the trapper let go the rifle. It fell on the soft grass in the clearing with scarcely a sound.

'That's better,' murmured Harbinger. 'Now you're showin' a little sense. We've got no quarrel with you, only with one man. Hand him over to us and we'll be on our way and you'll never see any of us again.'

'And if we don't?'

'Then we'll take him and make things bad for you.' There was a note of menace in the marshal's tone. 'It's your choice.'

'We got nothin' to tell you.'

It wasn't unexpected. From the moment he had ridden into this place and seen these men, Harbinger had guessed that this would be the outcome, had known what the ultimate was to be.

Harbinger paused for only a moment. Then he turned in his saddle to face Morando. 'Check the cabins. You help him Adams. If any of these *hombres* make any move to stop you, use your guns.'

'You can't shoot them down in cold blood,' put in Macey. His face seemed strained in the faint wash of sunlight that flooded the clearing, filtering down through the trees.

'I can if they don't tell me what I want to know.' Harbinger's tone was hard. 'I'm lookin' for a killer. If these men hide him, if they try to obstruct me, then they're goin' against the law and as such they're accessories.'

'It might be that if we explained things to 'em, they'd change their minds,' suggested the other.

Harbinger said nothing, but sat tall and still in the saddle, his hands resting loosely on the saddlehorn. It was almost as if he had forgotten the trappers, was concerned only with Morando and Adams as they moved from one hut to another, moving inside, then reappearing a few moments later, shaking their heads before moving on to another. So far, none of the watching trappers had made any move to prevent them. But there was a stillness in the clearing which Macey did not like. He eyed Harbinger with a worried air. He did not doubt that the man would hang one of these trappers just to make an example of him to the others, to force them to talk.

Adams and Morando came back. 'Nobody there,' said the half-breed, 'but

I figure there's one of the horses missin'.'

Harbinger sucked air in through tightly-clenched teeth. He lowered his severe gaze on to the man who stood before him. 'Of course,' he said thinly: 'Gardner would need a mount. He lost his, probably back there in the river.' He nodded his head ponderously. 'So he had to get one here and to my way of thinkin', he didn't have to steal it like a thief, he had it given to him. Helpin' a wanted man to escape like that is a criminal offence.'

'What do you mean to do about it?' asked Morando. He ran the tip of his tongue over dry lips.

'The same as I'd do to any other man who broke the law,' said Harbinger dully. He pointed to the trapper, standing in front of him, with his rifle lying in the grass at his feet. 'Take that man and hang him.'

'You can't do that,' broke in Macey. He urged his stud forward until he was level with the marshal. 'That badge of yours doesn't give you the right to hang any man you please.'

'This badge gives me the right — and the duty — to keep law and order in any State,' said Harbinger without even bothering to turn his head to face the other. He did not take his hard-eyed gaze from the trapper's face. 'I said hang him. Morando! Get him up on to your mount. The rest of you watch those other men. If they make a move for their guns, shoot them.'

'This is murder,' protested Macey. His face was white, the muscles of his cheeks working under the tight flesh. 'I want no part in it.'

'You turnin' yeller, Macey?' snapped Harbinger. 'If you didn't like this job, you should have pulled out when the others did back in the mountains.'

'I didn't know you meant to hang innocent men just to catch up with this *hombre*, Gardner,' replied the other.

One or two of the men nodded in agreement with him. Some added a word in support of what he had said.

Harbinger waited until they had all finished, then motioned Morando forward. Slowly, ponderously, he straightened himself in the saddle. 'So you reckon these men are innocent.' His tone was a dull, harsh sound, heavy with sarcasm and ridicule. 'I've met up with men like these. They do everythin' in their power to baulk the law. If we give 'em half a chance, they'll turn on us and shoot us all in the back. That's the kind of men they are. Force is the only thing they understand.' He backed his mount a few paces, held his hands rigid above the gunbutts and faced the group. 'I've heard enough from you all. If you want to argue, then go for your guns, damn you!'

For a long moment, they looked silently at the man, all except Morando. The half-breed had already dropped from the saddle, was moving towards the edge of the clearing, to where the trapper stood, his bearded face tight but still defiant. One after another, the possemen turned their faces away.

160

Macey lowered his gaze reluctantly, stared down at the ground in front of him, not even lifting his head as Morando thrust his Colt hard into the bearded man's chest, forcing him towards the waiting horse.

'Mount up!' he said harshly. There was no argument, only those two words, bit out between his teeth. Slowly, the man swung up into the saddle. There were some angry mutters from the trappers clustered in a tight group in the middle of the clearing, but both Morando and Harbinger ignored them.

A thin, vicious smile tugged at the corners of Harbinger's mouth as he watched the half-breed take his riata from where it was lashed on to the saddle, make a loop and drop it neatly over the man's head, tightening it a little about his neck. When this was done, he lashed the other's wrists behind him, coiled the end of the riata in his hand and glanced up at the low overhanging branch of the nearby tree.

Out of the corner of his vision, Harbinger caught the sudden movement among the group of men several yards away. The trapper's hand dropped to his middle with the speed of a striking rattler. He had the long-bladed knife half drawn from his belt, but simultaneously with the warning flash in his head, Harbinger snatched at his gun, squeezed off one shot, the echoes from the muzzle blast running under the trees in a tumultuous racket, atrophying slowly in the distance.

The man clutched at his stomach, the knife slipping from fingers which no longer had sufficient life to keep a grip on it. He jack-knifed violently and pitched forward on to his face in the long grass. The stink of burnt powder was suddenly strong in the clearing. Morando's horse shied at the sudden explosion, quietened quickly as the other caught at the bridle. Then, with a quick, true cast, the half-breed sent the end of the riata spinning over the branch, caught it as it fell on the other side, lashed it to the trunk and stepped back.

'You still got nothin' to say?' called the Marshal tautly.

For a moment, the other did not move. Then he twisted his head around with a wrench of his neck and shoulder muscles. He drew his lips back over his teeth, and there was a deep anger in his voice as he rasped out: 'You claim that you're a lawman, but you're worse than the man you're huntin'. Even if you kill me and ride on out of here, these men will spread your name over the face of Colorado. There'll be no room on the desert for any of you. Remember that when you try to ride out after him.'

Somehow the other managed to draw himself upright in the saddle: somehow he faced the other without any fear on his face. If there was any expression there at all, it was anger and defiance. It purpled his face, distended the veins in his neck and drew a hazy film down over his narrowed eyes.

Harbinger shrugged. The other's

words did not seem to have touched him. He gave a quick nod to Morando. Drawing back his arm, the half-breed slapped hard on the horse's flank. It leapt forward with a sudden lunge, the rope tautened, and the deed was done.

★ ★ ★

Harbinger turned to look at the faces of the men around him. His own features were hard, mask-like. Macey's horrified glance was fixed on the body which swung on the end of the rope, no longer jerking, but very still. He seemed to be finding it difficult to put his thoughts into words.

'Well, Macey,' murmured Harbinger, very soft.

The thin man shook his head. Almost, it was as if he had not heard the other man's words. Then he pulled on the wide brim of his hat, licked his lips and said harshly: 'That was nothin' short of murder, Harbinger. I've ridden along with you so far because I figured we were on the trail of a man who's been proved to be a killer. I didn't stop to ask questions like Condon and the others did back there. I figured you were in the right. Now I'm no longer sure about that. Anybody who'd string up an innocent man like that just for not talkin', ain't the sort of man I care to ride with. I'm pullin' out right now.'

Harbinger stared at him unblinking. 'You stayin' here?'

'That's right. Then I'm headin' back to Nebraska. Reckon I should've done that a while ago.'

'That goes for me too.' Kelly moved his mount forward until he stood beside Macey. One by one, other men gigged their mounts forward.

Jeb Harbinger's hard glance spread over them like a wave, touching each man with his scorn.

'Then stay here, damn you!' he roared. 'I'm goin' on after Gardner.' His lips tightened, compressed into a hard line. 'What about you, Morando? Do you stay with these yeller-livered curs?'

The half-breed shook his head. 'I started out on this ride, I'll stay with it, Marshal,' he said.

'I'll ride on,' broke in Adams.

'And I,' Keene gave a quick nod, moved out of the main bunch of men. He hitched his gunbelt a little higher, the slanting rays of the sun showing on his tight-drawn face.

Two other men, Mannix and Holliday, moved to join the small group. The other men did not move. Harbinger eyed them narrowly for a long moment, eyes glittering under the thick, black brows. 'Get out of my sight,' he hissed. 'I'll find Gardner without you and bring him back like I swore I would.'

His hand jerked fiercely on the reins, pulling the great horse's head around. His heels dug deep into the animal's flanks, as he sent it racing out of the clearing and along the narrow trail which led deeper into the trees. The five men followed him in single file, riding out without a single backward glance.

The trail ran out through the trees,

played out through gravel and large chunks of rock to the desert's edge. The sandy plain had a bright glow with the sunlight lying on it. Harbinger heard hard gravel churn under his horse's feet and the animal stumbled once, righted itself with an effort as he pulled it on, coming soon to better footing.

He thought disgustedly of the other men, refusing to ride with him because he had done the only thing open to him in the circumstances. He felt no regret for having hung that mountain trapper. The man had been holding something back from him, had probably been the one who had taken Gardner in for shelter in the first place, possibly tending his injuries, healing his wounds and then giving him a horse and provisions so that he could continue his flight from the law.

Morando moved up until he was beside him, his horse matching the Marshal's stride for stride. The half-breed's eyes were slitted against the glare of the sunlight reflected from the vast bowl of the desert and his lips were thinned as he said: 'Those hillbillies could still mean trouble for us, Marshal. They won't forget what you did back there and they may come after us.'

'If they do, we'll get plenty of warnin' once we're out there in the desert.' Harbinger pointed, not unduly worried by the possibility.

Morando's eyes remained speculative. 'If they wanted to do it,' he went on, 'they might do it before we get there.'

The answer to that came from the stunted trees that lined the high rocks to their right. On top of Morando's remark, the rifle shot whined down, kicking up the flinty shale almost directly between the two men. As if that solitary shot had been a pre-arranged signal, a volley crashed down on them. Mannix gave up a loud cry, lifted a hand to his chest, struggled to remain upright in the saddle, but couldn't make it. Without a further sound, his body arched and a trickle of blood oozed from between tightly-clenched teeth. Slipping sideways, he hit the ground like a sack of grain, lay still as his mount bolted along the twisting trail.

'Take cover,' yelled Harbinger. He dropped from the saddle, grabbing at his Winchester as he fell, rolling several times until he ended up behind a tall, rough-hewn boulder. A bullet chipped a piece of stone from it, sent it singing past his ear. A second bullet broke ground to one side of him and a third one ricocheted with a murderous whine off the boulder just above his head.

Now that he was under cover, he had the chance to place the gunfire. It was almost all coming from the low trees which bordered a steepish rise about a hundred yards away. They were fortunate that only Mannix had been hit. The trappers had moved quickly, possibly by some route known only to themselves and had taken him completely by surprise. If that sniper hadn't been so trigger-happy, a swift volley might have emptied every saddle. He lay a minute catching his breath, then worked his way slowly to the edge of the boulder. There was a deadfall lying over to his left and a sudden red tongue of flame erupted from it without warning. He felt the wind of the bullet as it passed within an inch of his face, withdrew his head quickly. The rifleman was on the opposite side of the dead fall and able to pin him down. Rolling swiftly to the other side of the boulder, he flattened himself behind it, seconds ahead of another bullet.

Savage reports of gunfire came from all around them now, great shouting echoes muttering through the trees, bouncing off the rocks so that it was impossible to tell accurately where a man lay hidden unless the muzzleblast could be seen. In the strong sunlight, this was not always possible.

Pressing his chest down on to the hard, flinty ground, he wriggled forward around the base of the big rock and waited with his eyes glued on the distant deadfall. He ignored the rest of the crackling rifle fire, leaving the other men to deal with it. The unknown trapper over there had to show himself in order to fire, he reasoned. And if he could spot the sudden movement quickly enough, he might be able to get his own shot in first. It was a long wait. Gunfire roared from all about him as he lay there, eyes glued on the place where he knew the gunman to be. He guessed that the other four men had reached cover without being hit for there was still a savage volume of return fire crashing into the trees where the main body of the trappers lay.

Relinquishing the long-barrelled rifle, Harbinger withdrew one of the Colts from its holster, swiftly checked the chambers, then made a rest with his left arm, sighted the gun on the spot where he expected the hidden man's head to appear, ready to fire the instant that the other showed so much as a faint blur of white to mark the position of his head.

Carefully, he let his gaze wander over the whole length of the deadfall, watching the spot where the branches had been snapped and shattered by the fall. His trigger finger tightened a little around the curved steel of the trigger, ready to squeeze off a series of rapid shots. Something moved, very slowly and cautiously. He felt the muscles under his breastbone tighten. The man's head lifted stealthily from behind the spreading roots of the tree. He had obviously lost sight of Harbinger, was trying to pick out his hiding place once more. The marshal waited for a split second, for perhaps the space of a single heartbeat, then squeezed down on the trigger, loosing off a couple of shots. The head jerked back, then vanished. Harbinger thought he heard a faint cry from behind the deadfall, but in the savage lash of rifle fire, it was impossible to be sure of what he had heard. When the head did not reappear, he took it that at least one of his shots had struck home. He listened critically for a moment, thought it probable that the men with him were holding their own, that now the advantage of surprise no longer rested with the trappers, the gunfight was going slowly, but surely, in their favour.

For several minutes the blind-firing continued. It soon became clear that this fight would not result in casualties unless the men involved became a little careless for there was plenty of cover for both sides and these men were all seasoned gunfighters, not likely to take chances. After a few more minutes the firing dribbled away into an ear-ringing silence, a kind of deep hush which made a man's nerves crawl. Harbinger fought down the urge to spring to his feet and run towards the distant trees, shooting from the hip as he ran. In the stillness, he listened tautly for any sound of movement from the men among the trees, heard nothing for a few moments, then picked out the faint crackle of twigs being crushed underfoot.

At the same moment, Morando's voice called: 'They're pullin' out, Marshal. I figure they've had enough.'

Harbinger eased himself to his feet. He could picture the mountain men moving back through the stunted trees. Pressing close to the boulder, he shifted the Colt into his left hand, edging forward. It was his intention to advance on the trees and try to cut off the men before they could slip back to the clearing. He did not get the opportunity. A high-ranging bullet, cutting out from the distant trees, struck the boulder close beside him, ricocheted with a thin, high-pitched scream through the air and caught him on the side of the temple. There was a violent explosion in his brain and then blackness as he pitched on to the hard ground like a dead man, lying still as Morando came running towards him . . .

When he came round, his head throbbing savagely, his vision strangely blurred as he forced his eyes open, he twisted his head slowly from one side to the other, trying to focus his vision, to see where he was. That was when he heard Adams's voice saying softly:

'He's comin' round, Morando. Reckon it'd take more than a creased scalp to finish him.'

Vaguely, he was aware of someone moving towards him, looming high over him, a hazy figure, features wavering as he tried to push his sight through the red haze of pain. Morando went down on one knee beside him.

'How are you feelin' now, Marshal?' he asked.

With an effort, Harbinger forced himself up on to one elbow, touched his head with the fingers of his other hand. There was a smear of dried blood just beneath his ear. 'What happened?' he asked tightly.

'Bullet shaved your scalp,' said the other quietly. 'Another inch and you'd be dead.'

Sucking in a sharp gust of wind, he sat upright, wincing as agony passed through his skull, lancing into his brain.

He saw that they were no longer among the rocks, but in the desert, close to a dried-up waterhole.

'We brought you out here,' Morando said. 'Those critters were headed back for more men and we reckoned there was no sense in stickin' around to argue with 'em any more. We should be safe enough here until you can travel.'

5

Killer Marshal

A small fire burned brightly on the edge of the wide Colorado River. Squatting close beside it, Rob Gardner chewed the strip of beef reflectively for several seconds before letting it slide down his throat. He washed down his supper with cold water from the river, then settled himself back against the over-turned saddle, easing his aching shoulders into the rounded half-curve of the leather. He felt almost too tired to sleep. Overhead, the round face of the Utah moon, huge and yellow, floated serenely and majestically into the clear sky, turning the surrounding country into a dull wash of light, cold and eerie, with most of the nearer details cleanly picked out from the darkness of the overall background.

For a moment he stared off into the

deep blackness which lay behind him, eyes narrowed as if he could see the man who rode after him, provided he could push his sight far enough across those limitless wastes. A week, a month — what did time matter when a man such as Jeb Harbinger was on your trail, determined to gun you down the moment he caught up with you? He knew that he had to keep riding west, setting a backbreaking pace for his mount. He turned his gaze to where the horse stood slack-legged, a dark shadow in the flooding moonlight. It had carried him well over some of the most terrible country ever encountered by him; vast stretches of sandy desert, interspersed by deep canyons which dwarfed his imagination. Out there, he had felt a loneliness and an utter silence which he had scarcely known could exist, a stillness so deep that it was almost as if one could hear the voice of God speaking out over the whole of Creation, with the brilliant stars standing out like foam in the yeasty ferment of the illimitable heavens. For countless miles he had ridden without seeing any sign of Man. These were the great wildernesses, wild and untamed, unaltered since the beginning of Time. Nature had done things in a tremendous way out here and men seemed puny creatures when compared to this great new country. A blunt finger absently traced a design in the sand near his right hand. He had covered close on forty miles that day, but he knew with a sense deep within him that it wasn't enough. For the first time, he started to think seriously of what would happen on the day of reckoning; when Harbinger and those men he had managed to keep with him, came face to face with the man they were hunting.

He yawned, settled back into the curve of the saddle, wriggling his shoulders a little to find a comfortable position. His chest was almost completely healed now, thanks to the attentions of Sam Freeman. Remembrance set him thinking of the old trapper, wondering what would happen to him once Harbinger came riding through that small, isolated community, asking questions and demanding answers. Harbinger would know that he had been there. He would probably have found the carcass of that cougar he had killed near the pass, would have followed his trail over the river, knowing that he was on foot once he had crossed the river, that the trappers were the only ones who could have helped him. Harbinger was utterly ruthless and there was no telling how far he might go if these men refused to tell him what they knew.

But there was no use in thinking about that now. His eyes closed and sleep came in to the faint rhythmic sound of a coyote wailing out in the desert, lifting its voice to the moon.

With the daybreak, he rode out of his camp and by mid-morning came upon the first sign that men had been in this country before him. Looking down the steep slope he could see deserted mine works, the long ore tailings and the deeply furrowed gravel piles which stretched down the slope in long humps and just beyond them, the upper part of a half-ruined main shaft scaffolding. This had obviously been a big place in its heyday. There were the cyanide vats where the gold was extracted from the ore, standing close beside the crushing mills. But now everything was dilapidated, had that air of having stood alone and empty for many years.

Gardner felt the muscles draw tight under his ribs. The desolation of this place had a powerful effect on him, made him realize the utter futility of what he was trying to do. No man had ever succeeded in getting away from Jeb Harbinger, the Killer Marshal. What chances did he have? Would it not be better to stand and fight than to keep on running like a hunted animal? But there was no place where he would have a chance in hell of beating off Harbinger and the posse he had with him.

He resisted the urge to stay here for a

while and give his mount a chance to blow. The sun beat down on him from the flat, cruel mirror of the sky and there was little shelter down there except in one of the huts which still bore some semblance of a roof on the rotting timbers. But he knew, from his own experience, that there would be no water down there and his canteen was less than one third full. It was imperative that he should find water before nightfall or he could not last another day on this terrible trail.

The trail, obliterated in places by wind-drifted dust, came narrowly in from the topmost ridges and entered the flat once more. It moved across a wide plain which had been still and quiet until he came on to it and then a sighing wind sprang up, throwing dust into the air, filling it with countless millions of stinging, biting grains of alkali that blotted out the full light of the sun, leaving it as a dull fiery redness through the writhing fog. It was impossible to move through the storm.

He crouched down behind his mount, his jacket pulled high over his head in an attempt to shield his face, but in spite of this, the questing grains managed to work their way into his mouth and eyes and ears. White dust poured in tiny rivulets from his body and his mount struggled to get to its feet, beginning to panic as he held desperately on to the reins to keep it still.

Not until the sun shone clearly again, did he dare to move. Wiping the mask of dust from his face, he got unsteadily to his feet, looked about him. The trail had been wiped clear by the drifting dust and sand. Off to the north, the grey-white cloud was moving away and all about him, the wind died as suddenly as it had sprung up. He stretched his numbed limbs, feeling the sharp stabbing agony of cramp. Overhead, the blue of the sky came back and he lifted himself wearily into the saddle. His throat seemed clogged by the vile dust, but he dared not use any of the water in his canteen to wash it away. The desert seemed to stretch in front of him for miles with no sign of a waterhole.

Feet sinking deeply in the treacherous sand, his mount picked its way forward, head low. It was almost at the limit of its endurance, he thought grimly.

Five miles, then five more. At last, he found the trail again where it swung south for a way before turning west again. Sharp-spined devil's club grew on both sides. The sun was high, shining directly into his eyes and he rode stiff in the saddle, horse and man forming a tiny speck of humanity on the vast spread of the desert.

He moved along the lee of hills that threw back the burning heat of the sun, the very earth seeming ready to crack with the high temperature. It was almost too hot to sit in the saddle and the horse was so exhausted that it could scarcely toil its way up the slippery slopes. Laying a trail of dust across the mesa, he rode as the sun moved down towards the western horizon and the air became cardinal with light reflected down from the towering buttes of sandstone. Awed a little by the vastness of the place, by the tomb-like silence, he skirted one of the buttes that stood up from the plain like a great landmark, put down by some Creator to mark the passage of time in this great, open space, where even time seemed to have little meaning.

Rob's face was shiny with sweat, itching with the caustic dust which lined it, and his eyes searched the hungry distances, striving to pick out some waterhole where he might replenish his meagre supplies. It was time for him to rest too, but not out here on the mesa where both man and horse could die of the bitter cold, where there was neither food nor water.

It lacked an hour to sundown when he reached the edge of the mesa and rode down a steep slope into a basin where a faint wind sighed up at him, sweeping the air clean of dust. It brought too, the smell of water and the horse picked up its gait, stepped it out a little more quickly now, its nostrils distended. Standing in the stirrups, to ease the ache in his legs, he looked out into the growing darkness. The sun went down like a penny going into a black box. The reds and golds vanished swiftly, the twilight lingered for brief moments only, and then the blues of the night crept in and swamped all other colours of the spectrum.

He rode for perhaps half an hour in the darkness before reaching water; a narrow, muddy creek that flowed down a steep slope close beside the trail. The water tasted of the brown-red mud, but it was drinkable and he drank until his belly could hold no more, filled his canteen to the brim, then let his horse drink. In a small dry-gulch, he made a fire of greasewood and scrub, sat hunkered on his heels beside it, letting the warmth of it soak into him. Here, with scarcely a cloud in the heavens, with the stars having a brilliant, diamond-like glitter, the heat of the earth dissipated swiftly into the night air and the temperature dropped well below freezing during the nights. He rested for a moment, then got up, hobbled his horse, and went in search of more wood and brush for the fire. Harbinger, wherever he was, would have to rest also and he knew he could afford to make camp here so long as he rode out at first light.

The horse grazed in the coarse, tough grass which grew at the edge of the gulch and was quiet. Laying his blankets close to the pyramid of the fire, he fed more wood on to the cracking, leaping flames, then lay down with the blanket pulled up to his neck, watching the train of red sparks as they lifted from the fire, climbed into the air and were then caught by the vagrant breeze and whirled away over his head.

★   ★   ★

Jeb Harbinger and the four possemen reined up and rested on top of the high ridge which looked down on to the old, deserted mine workings. They had reached this point five days after Rob Gardner had passed that way, but they did not know that. There were no trees here, no scrub, merely some tuftweed dotted here and there growing out of the thin layer of arid soil, the roots digging down to find what little moisture there was lying below the surface. Further on, the men had noticed the mesa in the distance.

While Morando lit a fire with handfuls of the tuftweed and pieces of wood which they fetched up from one of the ruined buildings down in the deep valley, Harbinger walked out to the edge of the long ridge and stared out to the west, where the last red rays of the setting sun lay on the desert, painting it with long black shadows, giving the ground a mottled appearance.

Adams came up to him, stared ahead

and then began to search the ground from side to side. 'He came this way?' he asked softly.

Harbinger moved his head slowly. He straightened his shoulders a little. 'Yes, Adams. He came this way.'

'How far ahead is he now?'

'Four, maybe five days, I guess.'

'How far are you goin' when we do catch up with him? You really mean it when you say you'll shoot him down in cold blood without givin' him a chance?'

The other touched the bandage around his forehead. 'I'm goin' all the way with Gardner,' he said tensely. He looked back to where the others had the fire burning in a shallow hollow. He knew that Morando had no compunction about killing a man. The half-breed was one man he could really trust to back him the whole way. As for the others — well he wasn't quite as certain about them. They had stuck with him in spite of two setbacks. But that did not mean they wouldn't turn and leave him if the going got really tough.

'You going to be the judge in this case?' asked Adams softly.

Harbinger stared down at him for a long moment. When he spoke, there was an absolute lack of emotion in his tone. 'I'm goin' to be the judge and the executioner.'

Adams glanced at the guns in the other's holsters, then nodded. 'I'd sure hate to be in Gardner's shoes when we do find him,' was all he said.

They turned and went back to the fire, a faint glow in the whole of the dark wilderness. Later that night, lying in his blankets, listening to the faint soughing of the wind among the rocks and the crackle of the flames as they ate their way hungrily through the fresh branches which had been tossed on to the fire, Harbinger felt some of the bitter frustration return to his mind.

All of these long days on the trail and still nothing to show for it but a saddle-weary body and a bullet's crease along his scalp. Tomorrow they would continue the seemingly endless ride, still heading west into an inhospitable country. He pushed the idea from his mind, rolled over on to his side and closed his eyes, drifting off into sleep to the sound of the licking flames . . .

★　★　★

Rob Gardner crossed into Nevada at a point just west of the Virgin River, knew that he could not run much further. Somewhere, there had to be a turning point for him and the sooner he reached it, the better. He rode up over the edge of a brown, crumbling dry-gulch that had once been a river bed in long ages past but which was now nothing more than a depression in the sun-baked earth, a stream of dust and smoothly-rounded pebbles with one or two larger boulders scattered here and there. His mount hesitated for a moment as the earth moved beneath its weight. Rob sat swiftly forward in the saddle, easing his long body over the animal's neck while it strained and heaved, panting, its ears pricked forward, pebbles and rocks cascading from beneath its hoofs as they moved towards firmer ground at the bottom of the depression. Then it shook itself loose from the tight rein and made its way forward while Rob pushed his wide-brimmed hat further forward on his head to shield his eyes from the glare of the flooding sunlight. It had been a long journey since he had set out from Nebraska with that posse on his heels, but here the country was better than that which he had just crossed. It was as if a harsh and relentless Nature had suddenly repented. Ahead of him, a range of low hills lifted from the yellow-grass plain, their peaks not very high and smoothly rounded, unlike the tall, steep mountains he had been forced to cross in his flight westward. Far over on his right, their peaks still capped with white there were mountains, but so distant that they had gathered a purple mist about their lower slopes and even the crests shimmered in the heat. He rubbed his forehead wearily, felt the sweat lying on his flesh and wiped it away with the back of his hand. He had ridden too many flaming days through, seen too many deep-silenced nights full of majestic, flaring stars for it not to have made an impression on him. Even outwardly, it had laid its touch on him, his skin burned brown to almost the same shade and texture of old leather and his eyes were permanently lidded, the flesh around the corners wrinkled from being screwed up against the vicious sunglare for so long.

He had crossed mighty rivers in flood, ridden over stretching deserts with not enough water to cool his parched throat or wash away the stinging, foul alkali dust that gathered on a man's body and in his throat. The trail had led him through dense forests, thin-leafed cotton-woods or the deep green of conifers, over rapid-running streams and over some of the most desolate country in the world. He thought back to the high bluffs, the great ravines whose naked, sun-painted sides had glowered down at him as he had ridden through them, the bluffs which had lifted clear to the wide open heavens with the arroyos lying deep among them. Such was the country through which he had ridden for more than twenty sun-scorched days, where the great sandstone mesas had dwarfed him and his mount completely and utterly so that he had grown to look upon himself as some insignificant speck on the vast map which was this part of the United States. Someday, maybe, men with an imagination and a determination greater than his, might come out here and change the varied artistry with which Nature had created and carved this land out but until then the only tools that would shape it were the wind and the rain and the sun. There had been more nights of cold and days of heat than he cared to remember; and although he had not realized it at the time, the days had worked their effect on him too, changing his subtlety from the raw, simple-thinking man who had ridden out of Twin Creeks, knowing that there would be a posse on his trail within days. Then, he had thought little about Jeb Harbinger, beyond the fact that he was, perhaps, the most ruthless lawman in the entire territory, that once he got his teeth into anything, he refused to let go. Now, he had fallen into the way of looking upon Harbinger as his enemy, as a man who could be killed, just as any other man could die.

Sooner or later, he would be forced to turn. Very soon, he would say to himself: This is far enough. Still he had seen no sign of life out here, yet there would be some habitation close by. With land as good as this, it was certain that someone had come along and had settled here.

Midday came and went and still he did not halt his mount. Not until halfway through the long afternoon, did he stop and draw rein. Sliding to the ground, he loosened the cinch and let the horse nibble at the green grass which grew in profusion here. Sitting on his haunches in the shade of a tall tree, he made a cigarette, smoked it slowly, savouring the smoke in his lungs, mindful of the low hills still some miles ahead of him. With luck, he ought to reach them by sundown; make camp there and then ride on to the open ground on the other side.

When he eventually got to his feet, whistled the horse over and stopped to tighten the saddleband once more, the sun lanced directly into his eyes, striking the upper half of his face and he pulled the brim of his hat lower over his forehead. The horse snickered, stood ready as he flipped the butt of the cigarette away and climbed up into the saddle, easing himself into his accustomed position. The hills beckoned him in the distance, gleaming in the slanting sunlight, smooth and sharp and inviting. There would be good camping places there, he decided, urging his mount forward, anxious to reach them, knowing that the best part of the day had gone. Pressing his knees into the horse's flanks, he urged it on at a faster pace.

Several hours later, with the sunset flaming in the west, and the world around him poised on the edge of a deep, vast stillness, in a strange quality of light which was neither daylight nor dark, but something in between, he climbed a narrow, twisting trail through tall trees with scarcely any brush among them, and reined up at the top, making camp in a small clearing beside a narrow brook which rippled musically over smooth white stones, between sandy banks. Here, there would be shelter from the breeze that had sprung up with the setting of the sun and his fire would be seen neither by prairie dogs or any riders in the vicinity. It came to him as he sat in front of the fire that he would soon be approaching civilisation once more after the long journey across Colorado and Utah and he had no wish to entertain any unwelcome visitors.

Taking the saddle from the horse, he laid it down near the fire, then moved to the brook and washed the dust from his face and neck. His flesh stung as the mask of alkali cracked with the touch of the water and he rubbed himself dry with his neckpiece. By the time the flame had died from the sky and the first bright stars were visible through breaks in the overhead branches, he had made a meal, heated it and washed it down with water. He had lived on meagre rations for the past ten days and his belly never seemed to have ceased its gnawing hunger pains. It was a monotonous diet but one not of his own choosing. Perhaps the next day, he might be able to shoot himself a jackrabbit and have a taste of meat for a change. Until then, he would have to be satisfied with what he had. He ate slowly, then sat back and listened to the night sounds in the darkness. There was the unmistakable shivering wail of a coyote, but so far away that he could not judge distance and closer, among the branches, a night owl hooted a melancholy sound as something scurried through the bush on its nocturnal errand.

The darkness, the stillness and the starlight told him it was time to sleep. The warmth from the fire soaked into his body, relaxing taut muscles and easing the pain of cramp which came from being in the saddle far too long. He edged his feet out a little under the blanket and was asleep almost at once.

When he woke, it was still dark. There was a dull red glow from the fire a few feet away, an occasional brightening as the flames fed on a fresh piece of wood sending a fan of sparks high into the air among the lower branches and he judged that he had been asleep for perhaps two, maybe three, hours. He pushed himself up on to his elbows, straining his ears for the faintest sound. Something had woken him, had probed deep into that part of his mind which never slept. He tried to think what it could have been, waiting for the sound to repeat itself.

A taut, quivering silence hung over everything. The breeze had almost died completely. Getting warily to his feet, he kicked dirt on to the fire, killing it. Interest and caution were rising together in his mind as he buckled on his gun-belt, moved silently through the trees. A moment later, he heard the dull run of horses in the distance.

The silence of the hills had in it the tag-ends of other sounds, as if there were many riders out there, their trails criss-crossing in the darkness, but he concentrated on the sound of the nearby riders. They seemed to be on some other road or trail through the timber which appeared to be slanting in his direction for the sound grew greater, then reached a peak and began to fall off again when the men could not have been more than half a mile from his camp. It was unmistakably a band of night-riders pushing hard into the hills. His first thought, that somehow Harbinger and the posse had caught up with him he dismissed after a moment's reflection. They could not possibly have travelled as swiftly as that; and the desertland had been empty of riders for as far as the eye had been able to see shortly before sunset.

He waited tensely until the gentle abrasion died in the distance, then moved back into the clearing. He did not feel unduly worried. There was sure to be a ranch somewhere close by in this hill country, possibly where the low hills sloped down into the plains on the other side of the range. There might also be a town not far away and it was this thought which disturbed him a little more. It was just possible that his description had been wired ahead of him by telegraph and there would be a posse on the look out for him even here. Shivering a little, he sank down beside the fire, feeling the ache in his chest but knowing there would be no more sleep for him that night. He rolled himself a cigarette, smoked it slowly, then kicked at the ashes of the fire until a faint redness appeared and threw on a handful of twigs, blowing on them to fan the flames. The night air was cold, numbing his limbs and after a while he lay flat on his back, his head resting against the saddle, his feet to the fire, staring moodily at the glimmering stars in the yeasty ferment of the heavens.

Nearby his horse nickered shrilly, jerked up its head as if in sudden alarm. Swiftly, instinctively, he jerked himself up on one elbow, his right hand snaking towards his gun. It was almost clear of leather when a voice from the shadows on the edge of the faint firelight said harshly: 'Hold it right there, friend.'

Rob hesitated for a moment, then moved his hand away from the weapon, allowing it to drop back into its holster.

'That's better. Now get your hands lifted . . . higher.'

Coming up on to his knees, he raised his hands above his shoulders, tried to peer into the gloom, to make out the identity of the other. If it were one of the men riding with Harbinger, then better to make a try for his gun than to be taken alive, for he had no doubts as to what his fate would be once he fell into the Killer Marshal's hands. Narrowing his eyes, he waited. Boots crunched on the loose rocks beyond the firelight. Then two dark shadows came forward, spread apart a little, one much taller than the other. Both had guns in their hands.

'What do you want with me?' he asked slowly, his voice tight. 'If this is a hold-up you'll get little money from me.'

The taller of the two figures stepped forward. Hard-faced, with dust on his clothing, he glared down at Rob, lips thinned back. 'What's your name, mister?'

Rob thought fast. Maybe the other had heard of him, maybe not. Certainly he was not one of the posse or he would have recognized him at once, would have seen the picture which Harbinger carried with him.

One look at the gun held unwaveringly in the other's hand told him it would be useless to lie. 'Rob Gardner.'

'Where are you from, Gardner?'

Rob shrugged. 'You name it and I'm from there,' he said quietly.

The other stepped forward, kicked out with his boot. The tip caught Rob in the side, knocked him sprawling in the grass. Pain jarred redly through his arm and chest and he sucked in a sharp breath as he fell, eyes blurring with the pain. Out of the corner of his eye, he saw the other draw back his foot, knew that a second vicious kick was on the way and tried to roll away from it, wincing inwardly.

Before the blow landed, the other figure spoke sharply: 'That's enough, Luke! We can get what we want out of him without that.'

Rob felt a stab of stunned surprise go through him. It had been a woman's clear and resonant voice. With an effort, he rolled over on to his back, lay there, staring across the flickering glow of firelight, to where the girl had stepped forward a couple of paces, was now looking down at him in the dimness. Her hat was tilted back on her head and the chestnut curls had escaped from beneath it, framing her face like a gleaming halo where the firelight caught her. She wore a tan shirt and a dark riding skirt and even through his pain-blurred eyes he was able to see the smooth, lovely curve of her throat and the wide dark eyes that watched him now with unveiled suspicion.

'This is the only way to get the truth out of men like this, Miss Rose,' said the man harshly. 'If you try any other way, he'll say anythin' to get out of admittin' he's one of that bunch.'

'I'm a little puzzled as to why he's here,' went on the girl slowly. 'If he was riding with them, he would surely have pushed on into the hills and by the look of this fire, he's been here most of the night.'

The man was silent at that, then nodded in a grudging way. But his tone was still sharp and ominous as he repeated: 'Where are you from, mister? If you're not ridin' with that outfit of rustlers, then you've got nothin' to worry about.'

Rob sucked in a breath, rubbed his ribs. It felt as if they had been caved in by that vicious kick and each breath he took sent a stab of agony through him. 'Can I stand up?' he asked.

'You can get up,' said the girl. 'But don't try anything funny. Luke here is anxious to kill somebody for this night's work, and you could just be the one if you give him half a chance.'

'I don't know what you're talkin' about.' Rob eyed each of them in turn. He wondered how they had managed to get so close to him, without being seen. They must have spotted his fire through the trees even before he had heard that bunch of hard-running riders, and had left their own mounts some distance away, moving up stealthily on foot the rest of the way. But as yet, he had no idea what they wanted with him. It was clear they must have mistaken him for somebody else. But who? And what was this business they were talking about? With an effort, he got to his feet, stood with his hands lifted, looking at them.

'Unbuckle that gunbelt and let it fall real slow,' ordered the man harshly. The black hole of his gun muzzle did not move an inch, but remained levelled on Rob's chest.

Lowering his arms thankfully, Rob did as he was told.

'That's a lot better,' said the girl coldly. She let her gaze move around the camp, resting for a long moment on his horse near the trees. 'You look as though you've ridden a long way. Your horse is tuckered out, dusty too.'

He nodded. 'I've ridden far enough,' he admitted.

'How far?'

He paused, then shrugged. 'All the way from Nebraska.'

'Nebraska!' For a moment there was disbelief in the man's hard tone. He took a step forward. 'That's close on a thousand miles.'

'I know.'

'Then I reckon you must've had a pretty good reason for ridin' all that way. What is it? The law on your trail or somethin'?'

Rob rubbed his side. His body seemed on fire. Luke watched him closely, legs braced apart, the gun still in his hand.

'Whatever it is,' broke in the girl sharply, 'it's got nothing to do with our problem. He's just another trail-runner, maybe with the law close behind him, maybe not. He isn't one of the men we're looking for.'

Luke relaxed a little, 'Well . . . ' he began dubiously.

'Put up your gun,' ordered the girl quietly. She holstered her own, waited until the man had done likewise, then stepped forward, into the firelight. 'I apologise for this intrusion,' she said stiffly. 'But we had to make sure who you were.'

Rob breathed deeply. He said quietly: 'I gather that somethin' has happened tonight, somethin' to do with that bunch of riders who headed past here a little while back?'

Luke lifted his head and stared sharply at him. 'You heard riders?' he snapped.

Rob nodded. 'They woke me about half an hour ago. There must be a trail cutting through these hills about half a mile distant. They were on that, pushing hard into the hills.'

The other pondered that information for a long moment, then shrugged. 'No chance of catching 'em now,' he said tightly. 'There are a hundred trails in these hills and they could be miles away by now.'

'They shot three of our men, and rustled off a couple of hundred head of beef,' said the girl, by way of explanation. 'They've been plaguing us for nearly a year now, driving off our cattle, ambushing our men so that it's impossible to get anybody to work for us now.'

'Which ranch is this?' Rob asked.

'The Triple Diamond. These hills are the eastern limits. You're already camped on our range.'

'I figured this was open country. I guess I was wrong. I'll be ridin' on in the mornin' and — '

The girl eyed him speculatively, her eyes narrowed a little beneath the gently-curving brows. For a moment she debated within herself, then said quietly: 'Do you want a job? You'll find very little in Salema.'

'That a town?' Rob asked.

She nodded. 'About thirteen miles from here, over the hills and due west. If you want a job, saddle up and ride back with us.'

'Don't you figure you're bein' kinda hasty, Miss Rose,' broke in Luke. 'We don't know a thing about this *hombre*. He may have been posted here as a lookout by that rustling outfit. If we take him in and give him shelter, he could find out everythin' about us and pass on the information to those coyotes up in the hills. That way, you'd be playin' right into their hands. Besides — ' he paused, then went on meaningly, 'what's your Pa goin' to say about you hirin' a stranger like this?'

'I'll deal with my father when we get back,' said the girl, with an imperious lift of her chin. She moved away from the fire, her back to them for a moment and then swung back. 'Well, are you coming?'

'Sure.' Rob nodded, aware of the big man's hard scrutiny of him. He made up his blanket roll quickly, threw on the saddle, tightened the cinch, and strapped his roll to the saddlehorn. Giving the fire a kick with his boot, he stepped up into the saddle and rode out behind the two as they walked back along a narrow, winding trail through the trees, moving downgrade. Their mounts were tethered among the trees some three hundred yards from where he had made his camp.

As he rode beside them, out of the trees, down the slope of the hills and then out across the rolling plains which stretched west in the faint shimmer of starshine as far as the eye could see, he pondered on what his next move would be. If he took this job, it meant the end of his running. He would have to wait for the arrival of Harbinger and the posse and there would inevitably be a showdown. Whoever these people were who owned the Triple Diamond ranch, they would not step in and take his side, simply because he had agreed to work for them.

The moon, well past its third quarter, came up over the eastern horizon as they rode through the night. Rob glanced frequently at the girl out of the corner of his eye, studying her unobtrusively. At last however, as if feeling his glance on her, she turned her head and said softly: 'You'll find that this is an evil country, Mister Gardner. There are men in the hills who would destroy us if we gave them the opportunity. They rob us at every turn, they run off our cattle and kill the men we engage to work for us. Are you still sure that you want this job?'

Rob shrugged. 'You know nothing about me except my name, yet you've offered me work. For that I'm grateful. But maybe there are things you ought to know first.'

'Save them until you see my father,' said the girl softly. 'He will ask questions and he will know if you're lying or telling the truth.'

They rode in silence after that. A creek made a smooth run alongside the trail, a faint yellow gleam of reflected moonlight in the deeper darkness of the night. Then they rode up a gentle ride, across a flat area and on into a land of low hills and pastures.

Lights sparkled in the distance as they crossed a wide plank bridge over a sluggish river and ten minutes later, they drew rein in front of the ranch-house. Rob noticed the large circular corral and the three barns situated a short distance from the house itself. Then a light appeared in the doorway and a tall, broad-shouldered figure stepped down on to the porch, stared out into the darkness. There were other men near the far side of the courtyard, unsaddling their horses. Judging by the sweat and lather on the animals, these men had ridden far and hard and had arrived there shortly before they had.

The girl stepped forward beside him, said: 'We found this man near the East pasture, Dad, up in the hills. I'm afraid we mistook him for one of those raiders. He wants a job.'

The tall man laid a piercing glance on Rob, taking in everything about him. Then he said: 'Some strangers are welcome here, others are not. We must find out more about you before we decide what to do. I need honest men who are willin' to fight.' He glanced sideways at the man who had been with the girl. 'What do you think of him, Luke?'

'He's either one of that outfit from the hills, trying to lie his way out of a rope, or he's just another stray rider, runnin' from somethin' in his past. If he's that, then he's no good to you. He'll stay for a day maybe, perhaps a year, but there'll come a time when his past catches up with him and he'll run for the nearest hole.'

The other considered this, then jerked a thumb at the door behind him. 'I'll talk with him. If he came here with honest intentions, then the job is his. If not — well, we'll see.' He moistened his lips as he stood to one side and motioned Rob inside.

The girl touched Rob's arm as he stepped up on to the porch. 'I'll bring you some coffee and a bite to eat,' she said softly. 'I can see that you've eaten rough for some time.'

'I'd sure appreciate it,' he said gratefully. He stepped into the parlour with the tall, grey-haired man behind him. The other closed the door and pointed a finger at one of the chairs near the table. There was a lamp burning on the table, throwing yellow light into the corners of the room. Sinking down into the chair, Rob sat back, resting his shoulders, stretching his legs out in front of him. There was a dull ache in his side where Luke's boot had bruised his ribs and it still hurt whenever he drew in a deep breath.

'What were you doin' out there in the hills on my land?' The other watched him closely as he asked the question and something deep and enigmatic moved at the back of his eyes.

'I didn't know it was your land,' Rob said. 'I made camp there for the night. I figured there must be a ranch or a town somewhere close by, where I might get some work.'

'Cowhand?'

Rob shrugged. 'Well, it's honest work, I reckon.'

'But are you an honest man?'

'What do you mean by that?'

'You've got the look about you of a man on the run. A haunted look. I've seen it too many times in the past to mistake it. East of here, there's nothin' but desert and mountain, stretchin' clear through Utah and Colorado, all the way to Nebraska.'

'That's where I'm from,' Rob said simply. He saw the little gust of expression that went over the other's features, the slight tightening of the man's lips, the way his blunt fingers were intertwined in front of him, the knuckles white under the flesh.

'It's a long way for a man to ride, just for a job as a cowhand.' The other gave Rob a bright-black glance. 'Are you lookin' for somebody? Or is there someone back there somewhere, lookin' for you?'

When Rob hesitated, the other said: 'You'd better tell me the truth, mister. I can always tell a lie and you've got to admit, there are some peculiar circumstances here. You turn up on the border of my spread on the same night that the hill outfit kills three of my boys and runs off with a hundred head of prime beef. Even if there's no connection, it is a little strange don't you agree?'

'I guess it must look that way.'

'I like to go on a quick judgement of a man. My first impression of you is that you're an honest man. But if I'm wrong and you came here to spy on me, I'll shoot you down myself. Now, man, why are you here?'

'Does there have to be a reason?'

'There's a reason that drives every man,' muttered the other heavily. He glanced round as the door opened and the girl came in with a tray. She set it down on the table in front of Rob, and said: 'Go ahead, you can eat while you talk.'

Rob sipped the scalding coffee, felt it burn the back of his throat, but it brought a wave of expanding warmth in his stomach, made him feel better. There were freshly made scones too and a couple of soda cakes. He ate them ravenously and the grey-haired man said nothing until he had finished and both plate and cup were empty.

'Thank you kindly, ma'am,' Rob said, smiling up at the girl. 'I reckon I sure needed that.'

'Now,' said the tall man heavily. 'Let's get back to you. You followin' somebody or is there someone on your tail?'

Rob was acutely aware of the girl's level gaze on him. He shrugged, said finally: 'You ever hear of a man called Jeb Harbinger?'

He knew by the look on the man's face that the name was known to him. The other nodded. 'He's a United States marshal,' he said slowly. 'One of the worst kind of lawman. Reckons that the only good criminal is a dead one. That's why he takes every prisoner back over the saddle of his own mount. He was in Nevada some years back. Is he on your trail?'

'That's right. There was a bank hold-up in Twin Creeks, back in Nebraska. Two of the bandits and one of the bank guards were shot dead. The third outlaw managed to escape and make a run for it. I followed him out into the hills and then lost him. I was still huntin' around when the sheriff and a posse arrived and arrested me. There were plenty of men who swore they'd seen me outside the bank, that it was me who shot down the guard.'

'Go on,' nodded the girl.

'I figured that with all of this cooked-up evidence against me, I didn't stand a chance at any trial they rigged up for me. I knocked out the deputy when he brought my supper and broke jail, managed to get away into the hills. The sheriff couldn't follow me across the state line, but that wasn't goin' to stop Harbinger. He took up the chase with a posse he'd formed in Twin Creeks.'

'I see.' The other gave a tight-lipped smile. 'I've heard of Harbinger's reputation. He doesn't care whether a man is innocent or guilty, so long as he can hunt them down like an animal. And he's still on your trail?'

Rob nodded. 'He can't be more than two or three days behind me. How many men he still has with him, I don't know. Some of them may have given up and gone back home.'

'What do you think, Dad?' asked the girl, as the silence drew out in the room.

The rancher said nothing at the moment. He got to his feet and moved over to the window, staring out into the dark courtyard. He was still cool and suspicious. Rob watched his profile, saw the indecision which lay there. The other faced into the night and spoke to him from there. 'What would you do if Harbinger and his men were to ride in here — run away again, keep on runnin', or stand and fight?'

Rob licked his lips, knew the other was now prying him for his real worth, for his character. He said finally: 'I'm through with runnin' but I don't like bringing trouble to where I work.'

'Most of the men who've worked for me have had a past,' said the other slowly, picking and weighing his words with obvious care. 'I never asked them what it was, beyond the fact that if they were running from somethin' I needed them here. I'm sayin' the same to you. I want you to stay. I need every man I can get, men who can handle a gun. Hard men who will stand and fight when the showdown comes, whether it's against these rustlers or a man like Harbinger.'

Rob felt the tightness come to his face. The other had thrown him off balance by this remark. It was the last thing he had expected. Yet it made sense if one looked at it objectively. He held himself still, meeting the other's eyes as the man turned slowly, facing into the room. 'You might think that's a strange thing to say; but those in this territory who know Jeff Ovenden, know that he doesn't always judge a man's worth or his character by what he hears about a man's past. Even if there's truth in what the rumours say, a man's loyalty to me can outweigh a lot as far as I'm concerned.'

'But if Harbinger does come here he won't take no for an answer, even if you say so. He's a ruthless killer and if there's a crime committed any place that comes within his territory, he's got to have a prisoner. Are you big enough to stop him from ridin' in here and takin' me out?'

'Maybe. But I'm not here to protect you. You have to work out your own salvation. All I'm offerin' you is puttin' you up and a job. If there's trouble then it's up to you to find a way out of it. If you gun down Harbinger in fair fight, I'll testify to that and I reckon I can promise that you'll get a fair hearin' in town. We don't have any particular likin' for Harbinger or any of his kind around these parts.'

Rob nodded. 'That's as fair an offer as I've ever had, Mister Ovenden,' he said. 'I'll take the job.'

'Good.' For a moment there was an expression on the other's face which seemed to Rob to be one of relief. Then it faded and he grew brisk again. 'In return for that, I'll have men watchin' the trail from the desert. If Harbinger is on your trail, that's the way he'll have to come and you'll get warnin' of it, and also of how many men are ridin' with him.'

Rob held himself still, meeting the other's eyes. They were cool and hard; they knew him and yet they were puzzled, possibly wondering if he would step right up and fight when the chips were down, or if he would panic and run.

'The bunkhouse is across the courtyard,' Ovenden said. 'You'll find a bunk there and some blankets. In the mornin' we'll talk some more.'

The other turned down the lamp and went outside with Rob close on his heels. The moon drifted slowly over the southern horizon, lying low in the sky, a pale scratch of yellow against the foaming background of stars. There was still the smell of dust hanging in the air and several fresh horses in the corral. Ovenden must have several men on his payroll, he reflected as he made his way across to the bunkhouse. Why should the other give a job to a lame dog such as himself? Then he remembered the three men who had been killed that night near the Eastern Pasture, and guessed that Ovenden was merely trying to protect his own interests, building up enough men to throw back those hill people who continued to raid his herds.

Inside the bunkhouse, he found Luke seated at a long, wooden table with a deck of cards in his hands. The other glanced up, riffling the cards through his fingers. His eyes were hard and there was a curious expression on his bluff features. 'You get that job, mister?' he asked tightly.

'That's right.' Rob pegged his gear and found himself a bunk near the table, dropped his hat on to it, then straightened, looking across at the other. 'You still don't trust me, do you?'

'No,' muttered the other shortly. 'I'm the foreman here and it's up to me to check every man who joins us. We've had some killers in the outfit who went over to the rustlers whenever they found that the pickings were better on that side. We've had some who were always lookin' over their shoulders, jumpin' at their own shadow. They rode over the hill at the first sign of trouble. I don't want to see any more like that on the payroll. We have enough trouble with the hill crowd to worry about our own men.'

Rob smiled thinly at the other. 'You know damned well that I'm not one of the hill crowd.'

'Sure, I guess I was wrong about that. But your name and face sure are familiar if I could only remember where I've seen 'em before.'

Rob took his tobacco pouch from his pocket and began to build himself a smoke, seating himself on the edge of the bunk. There were several other men, lying on their backs, some snoring, others awake, reading or merely staring up at the ceiling over their heads. A handful watched him with interest.

'You ever been up in Arizona?' asked Luke softly, not looking up.

'No.'

'Along the California border then?'

'You've never seen me there,' Rob said quietly. He put a match to his smoke and drew deeply on the cigarette.

'Well by God, I've seen your face someplace,' muttered the other, his tone harsh. 'When it comes back to me, I guess I'll know all there is to know about you.'

'Why don't you ask Ovenden? He knows all there is to know,' Rob said calmly. He watched the other's face for his reaction, but it remained expressionless.

Finally, Luke nodded. 'I may do that,' he said at length. Getting up, he slammed the pack of cards down on to the table and moved off to his own bunk. 'It's gettin' late,' he said shortly, 'and it's been a long, hard night for all of us.'

Rob rubbed his hands together. The

warmth from the iron stove nearby suffused into his body and he stretched himself out on the bunk after taking off his gunbelt, his jacket and boots. One of the men got up, went forward and extinguished the lamp by running his cupped hand across the top of it. In the warm darkness, Rob lay for a moment, trying to think things out in his mind. So many things had happened in the past twenty-four hours that it was difficult to figure out what was best to do. He knew that he had now committed himself to staying here. After the help that Ovenden and his daughter had given him, and the promise to have men out watching the trail for the first sign of Harbinger and the posse, he knew that whatever happened, he could not run out on them. The die had been cast the moment the girl had offered him the chance of a job, back there in the hills. Lying there, he heard one of the men roll on to his side in his bunk and in the darkness, thinking about Luke and the other's animosity towards him, not trusting the man too far, he reached out and took both his guns from their holsters and slipped them under his pillow.

★　★　★

Back in the house, Rose Ovenden stood by the window of the dimly lit parlour, looking out into the darkness of the night, out to where the horses still milled around in the corral, then beyond them, up to where the low hills lifted on the horizon. Jeff Ovenden came in a few moments later, his face set in hard lines; a man lost in his own thoughts. He sank down into a chair at the table, with the lamplight etching his face with shadows and highlighting the planes of his cheeks. For a full minute he seemed unaware of his daughter's presence in the room, then he stirred himself and said quietly: 'I hope I did right, giving that young man a job.'

'I think you did, Father,' Rose said.

'He would be useful to us.'

'Almost any man would be useful to us now. We've got to stop these raids on the herd, or we'll soon be finished. Two or three hundred head every time they strike. Men killed or wounded. The men we have are not enough. Except for Luke, they're not the sort of men we want. They're afraid. They don't see why they should risk their lives to save what I've got. They'll run away, afraid of what the hill crowd will do the next time.'

'Do you think he was telling the truth, that he's innocent of this killing?'

'Perhaps. Does it really matter?'

Rose Ovenden drew herself up to her full height. She had dark eyes like her father, the same firm chin, the deep look of determination on her face. 'I think it could matter a lot,' she said eventually. 'I believe he's a good man, caught up in something which is not of his making. I wouldn't want to see him hurt by this Marshal Harbinger.'

'I've already said that I'll have the

boys watch the trail,' Jeff Ovenden said. 'What more can I do? He has to work out things for himself, although I'll do all I can to see that he gets an even break.'

'From what he says, he hasn't had one so far,' said the girl tightly. She walked slowly around the room. 'What kind of man is Harbinger?'

'He's a cold-blooded killer if the stories about him are true. He's never taken back a live prisoner yet. All have been killed, lying over their saddles when he brings them in.' The older man was silent for a long moment, sunk deep in his thoughts. Then he went on: 'I don't suppose there are many who would mourn for Jeb Harbinger if he was to be killed. But there would be awkward questions asked. After all, he's still a lawman and he's probably taken the trouble to carry a warrant with him authorising Gardner's arrest.'

'But if that evidence was framed,' protested the girl harshly. 'Or if they were to catch the real killer?'

'That would alter things a lot,' nodded the other. 'We'll just have to wait and see.'

'When are you going to set some of the men watching the trail?'

'First thing in the morning,' said the other. He drew in a deep breath, glanced at the clock against the wall. 'Time we got some rest now. And don't worry about Gardner. The way I see it, he'll have to face up to things now and that may be the making of him, the fork in the trail.'

6

The Warning

Rustlers are like vultures or other birds of prey, hanging in wide circles in the endless heavens; waiting for a chance to strike, planning every move before committing themselves, knowing that there was strength and death ranged against them, but depending on surprise, speed and utter ruthlessness to carry them through. Darkness was their friend; moonless nights, shadowed rocks, a savage burst of accurate fire which emptied saddles and sent men sprawling, dead, in the dust. But there were occasions when their plans failed, when they overlooked one particular, vital point, and paid dearly for their mistake. They made one on the night after Rob Gardner joined the Triple Diamond and rode out to the north pasture.

Luke and Rob Gardner slowed and walked their horses through the tumbled rocky ledges which overlooked the wide plain. Down below them, the herd milled contentedly, grazing on the rich, green grass that grew in profusion there. A river glinted in the dying sunlight and there were soft, purple contours spreading and smoothing the land. But here, among the rocks, the slanting sunlight cast stark harsh shadows that were hard on the eye. Tumbleweeds rolled in the dust that had gathered among the rough boulders and there were tall sky-rearing columns of rock which had been etched and fluted into weird, fantastic shapes by long ages of sun and wind and a bading sand. There was no sound here but the endless soughing of the wind, the crackling rustle as it bent the stiff leaves and spikes of the mesquite and thorn.

The utter desolation of the scene evoked no reaction in either man. Rob had seen it all before in his long journey across the deserts and mesas. Luke was sunk deep in thought, seeing nothing of the terrain around him. There was nothing here to bring pleasure to a man's mind, but it was a good place in which to fight, or to lie in ambush for men who might come riding down from the rising hills, to attack the grazing herd once darkness had fallen.

Shading his eyes with one hand, Rob turned in the saddle and surveyed the scene below them. There were men on horseback circling the herd, keeping it together with the coming of night, forming it into a large circle on the bedding grounds. The men knew that he and Luke were there, keeping an eye open for trouble, ready to lend the weight of their gunfire where it might be needed most if an attack did develop.

Rob indicated a tumbled heap of boulders a couple of hundred yards away, turned his mount towards them, the cautious animal picking its way carefully through the needle-edged rocks.

'Why are we stoppin' here?' demanded Luke harshly.

Rob turned. 'I figure this would be the best place to watch from,' he answered. 'We can see for miles from that point yonder and cut most of 'em down before they know we're here if they do happen to come along this trail.'

'And if they take one of the others?'

'Then we're no worse off.' He lifted his guns from their holsters, then let them slide back. Casting a quick glance at the heavens, he said softly: 'It'll be sundown in less than an hour. We'd better get under cover in case they're already movin' up among the rocks.'

'All right,' nodded the other grudgingly. He kneed his horse forward and a moment later they had dismounted away from the main trail, in a small rocky hollow among the high boulders. There was a bubbling stream kicking up a fine mist where it came out of the ground as a natural well and they drank of the cool water and settled back, moving their bodies to find a comfortable position. The wind died and the tumbleweeds rested. A deep and pendant silence lay over the rocks, and it was so still they were able to hear the plaintive lowing of the cattle far away in the valley.

The sun dropped swiftly as its flaming disc approached the horizon, turning the sky to flame and stretching a blanket of darkness over the valley. The hills kept some of the sunlight to themselves even after the sun had vanished and the tall peaks continued to shine while the rest of the world slumbered in darkness.

Soon, it began to grow cold and Rob pulled his arms tightly around his body in an attempt to keep in some of the warmth. There were many enemies out here in the hills. The cold, the silence, animals that slithered on their bellies and could sink their poisoned fangs into a man's leg before he knew they were there; not to mention the two-legged ones they were waiting for.

Sitting with his shoulders against a tall rock, Luke thrust shells into his guns, then thrust them back into his holsters. The silence stretched out and became eternal. The first of the sky-soldiers began to glitter in the heavens overhead.

'You think they'll come?' muttered Luke after a long pause. The sound of his voice in the stillness of the hollow sent little echoes rattling among the rocks.

'They'll come if they reckon they can get away with it,' said Rob. Deep down inside, he was hoping that the outlaw outfit would attack. It might ease the burning pressure inside his mind, might take his thoughts off the knowledge that now, perhaps only a day or two distant, Harbinger was nearing the end of his trail.

It occurred to Luke that Rob was, in spite of his outward appearance, both worried and insecure: and so he asked the same question again, this time in a voice that was little more than a hoarse whisper: 'Why do you reckon they'll come?'

'Very likely, because everythin' is in their favour. No moon until almost dawn and very little then, more cattle were pushed into this herd during the day, and after that attack on the south pasture only a couple of nights ago, nobody will be expectin' them to strike again so soon.'

'Well, if you're right, I hope to God they come soon. I'm perishin' here. It's so damned cold nobody could live up here.' The other shivered, got to his feet and crept towards the great curving boulder that loomed up against the night as a vast black shadow. 'Maybe we could light a fire for warmth. Nobody could see it in this hollow.'

'Don't be a fool!' Rob snapped. 'They'd not only see it, but they'd smell smoke a mile off and be warned.'

Luke straightened his hat. 'By the time they do come, I'll be so god-damned cold and numb, I won't be able to handle a gun.'

'You'll be all right.' Rob leaned back against the cold rock. He let his gaze roam about him, probing the rocks, the gullies and the climbing stretches of open ground across which he expected these rustlers to ride if they came this way. If they didn't then they would have to be doubly ready to move. The horses were tethered close by and they could be in the saddle within seconds, ready to ride out once they sighted these men.

The minutes ticked by now into an endless eternity, lengthening the night, accentuating the coldness which was all around them, in the ground, in the air, in their bones and in the chill brilliance of the stars over their heads. Down in the valley, the herders had lit two fires half a mile apart and the herd itself could just be been as a dark, sprawling mass in the valley, the great beasts quiet and bedded down for the night.

'They're not coming.' Luke heaved himself up on to one elbow, sat for a moment with his head cocked on one side, listening intently. The night was as still and silent as the grave. 'I tell you we're just sittin' up here wastin' our time for nothing.'

Rob felt the exhaustion, the deep chill, in his own body, knew the emotions which had prompted the other's remark. He said hoarsely: 'It's only about midnight yet. Give 'em time. They'll most likely be waitin' for the men down there to turn in, leaving only the guards at the herd, and they'll likely be dozing in their saddles.'

Luke muttered something under his breath, thrust his legs out straight in front of him to relieve the stabbing pains of cramp in his thighs. He rubbed the bristles on his chin, making a scraping sound which seemed oddly loud in the silence.

Rob looked coldly at the other. Was it fear which prompted him to act like this, the inability to remain calm under these trying conditions — or was he fuming under the strain of inactivity, longing for the enemy to put in an

241

appearance so that he might do something. It was quite impossible to tell from the other's attitude.

It was half an hour later, before they picked out the first rumour of sound high in the hills. At first, it was little more than a dull murmur at the very edge of hearing, but it gradually grew louder and resolved itself into the muted scrubbing sound of horses coming on at a swift pace. They were still, Rob judged, on the far side of the peak, probably making their way through heavy timber which would partly muffle the sound of their horses. As yet, they seemed to be making no attempt to disguise their presence there. He smiled grimly to himself in the darkness, reached out and touched the other's shoulder although he knew that Luke had heard them too. The other slid one of his Colts from its holder and held it meaningly in his right hand, feeling the balance of it, thumbing the hammer slowly.

'This is it,' murmured Luke softly.

He shifted his position cautiously. 'And they're headed this way.'

'Let them come,' Rob said thickly. 'We want them to move on past us without knowing we're here. Whatever you do, don't open fire until I give the word, or they'll fade back into the hills and we'll lose 'em again. We have to get them between the herd and ourselves. Once they open fire on the herders, we move in and take 'em from behind.' He was not sure that the other would obey this order when the time came but it was essential for the success of their plan that he should do so. He had tried to impress on the other the need to let the rustlers move by without trying to shoot any of them from their saddles. The two of them didn't have a chance of destroying this band. It would have to be a concerted effort, in conjunction with the men in the valley. By cutting off the rustlers' way of retreat, their chances of finishing this gang for good, seemed reasonably high.

The on-travelling murmur of horses

came closer, grew louder in the night, then stopped. Luke stiffened. He turned towards Rob, his face a pale grey blur in the darkness.

'They'll be at the summit of the hills now,' Rob said in answer to the silent query in the upraised brows. 'They won't want to give their presence away to anybody down in the valley, so they'll probably pussyfoot it down. Keep your eyes and ears open. We want to know where they are and how many of them before they draw level with us.'

Carefully, he inched towards the boulder that overlooked the trail leading down from the summit. He looked anxiously up into the deep shadows. Was there a movement in the distance, about half a mile away, a faint impression of men on horseback limmed against the skyline? He pushed his body flat against the rock, feeling a little tremor go through him as he realized that his eyes had not deceived him and even though it would be impossible for anyone up there to pick him out against the background, the tremor in his mind persisted. He heard Luke moving about in the hollow at his back. Then the first of the riders put his horse to the downgrade and the rest followed in single file.

Rob filled his lungs with air and stood absolutely still with his mouth open, letting the air go. The movement of the column on the trail was slow, snaking down through the rocks. There were moments when he lost sight of them, straining his eyes to pick them out again as they crossed a patch of more open ground. Then, almost before he was aware of it, the head of the column was a vague motion in front of them, coming on more swiftly than he had anticipated. He crouched down against the protecting boulder, glanced swiftly out of the corner of his eye, saw that Luke was flat against the base of one of the nearby rocks and let his breath go in slow pinches through his parted lips. The column moved by in the faintly glimmering starshine. Ten men riding with a singleness of design, a dark purpose, through the night. When they had moved by, rounded a bend in the trail some thirty yards away, he straightened up, motioned to Luke. Quietly, he made his way to his mount, swung up into the saddle. Luke did likewise and they delayed long enough for the murmur of sound from the rustlers to fade into the distance before edging their own mounts forward in their wake. The trail reached level ground and peering forward, Rob saw the column less than thirty feet below them.

Someone in the party said softly: 'They got a couple of fires burnin'. I figure it's time we moved in before they change the guard on the herd. That'd mean twice as many men awake.'

'Cal's right,' murmured another man halfway along the column. 'Hit 'em now and they'll have no chance. We did the same the last time and we must've dropped three or four of 'em. We can do the same again, believe me.'

Beside him, Rob felt Luke stiffen abruptly, felt the other's hand move down to his gun. Gripping the foreman's wrist tightly, fingers biting into the other's flesh, he forced him to stillness. It needed only something like this to start the other shooting and this was not the moment for it.

'All right. I don't want to be here by daylight anyway and we have to get the cattle up into the hills before dawn.' The harsh voice which spoke from the front of the column carried the weight of authority, 'Fan out and move in, but no shootin' until I give the signal. Everybody understand that?'

There were low murmurs of assent from the rest of the men. Then they began to move off once more, heading down the final slope which would bring them out among the tumbled rocks and boulders which divided the hills from the lush green valley.

'You ready?' Rob asked tightly, without turning his head.

'In case you haven't noticed, I've

been ready for almost half an hour,' said Luke sullenly. 'If you hadn't stopped me then I could've taken at least six of their saddles.'

'Maybe so. But that would have given the game away and we want to nail the lot. If you do as I say, we can do that. But you must have patience. Blind action will get us nowhere with this bunch.'

'Don't forget that Ovenden is down with the rest of the boys at one of the camps,' said the other thinly. 'If anythin' goes wrong, you'll be in trouble.'

'I know that.' Rob spoke through his teeth. Gently, he urged his mount around a bend in the trail, put it down a slide of loose gravel that moved treacherously under the horse's feet. There was a moment when he thought it would utter a harsh whinney of fear, warn the rustlers, but he reached forward swiftly and laid a hand over its nostrils.

The column had gone on. There was a brief rattle as they moved over the stones at the bottom of the slope. Then silence. Rob guessed they had ridden out on to the grass which would successfully muffle any sound and he felt the tension beginning to rise in great waves sweeping through his body, tightening the muscles of his chest and arms.

With Luke riding beside him, grim-visaged, they reached the valley, rode out slowly and silently, heading towards the nearer of the two fires. They could just make out the vague shapes of the riders now, an occasional man silhouetted against the flickering firelight as he moved across in front of the fire. Gently, Rob eased his Colts from their holster, rested his hands loosely in front of him. The signal from the leader of the hill people would not be long in coming.

When it did come, however, it came with the shock of the unexpected. A savage flash of flame against the blackness, the sound of the shot bucketing through the stillness.

Swinging a little, Rob saw that the others had fanned out more than he had thought and the shot had come from much further away, closer to the other camp than the one where most of the rustlers seemed to be.

Almost at once, uttering shrill cries, the rustlers rode their mounts forward, firing from the saddle. The answering fire from both camps was immediate, something none of the rustlers had expected. Outlined against the glare of the firelight, Rob saw one man throw up his arms and slide from the saddle, the fleeing horse, riderless now, vanishing into the darkness beyond the glow of the flames. Swiftly now, Rob urged his mount forward, digging in his knees as he used both Colts. Luke swung away to move around the rear of the wide arc of riders. The muzzle blast of his Colts lanced through the darkness in stilletos of flame. Another man uttered a loud cry somewhere in the blackness. More shots scattered the silence into echoing slivers of sound that shuddered and raced away into the vast distances.

The firing swung round. It seemed no longer to be pouring into the two camp fires, but from the direction of the herd. The sudden realization flashed into Rob's mind a second later. He yelled to Luke, pointed towards the milling shadow.

'They're tryin' to stampede the herd,' he shouted warningly. He swung his mount, headed towards the sprawling shadow which dominated the entire valley. Already, some of the men at the camp fires had realized the peril, were swinging up into the saddle, riding out swiftly. The three guards circling the herd were struggling to keep it together, knowing that once these great, unpredictable beasts began to stampede nothing on earth would stop them until they had run themselves out of wind.

Two dark shadows raced in front of Rob's vision, closing in on the herd, their guns splashing flame into the faces of the frightened animals. Rob aimed and fired in the same movement, saw one of the men clutch at his shoulder, sway in the saddle, grab for the reins and head off, away from the herd. The other swung sharply, drew up his gun. The bullet sang across Rob's shoulder. He jerked himself sideways in the saddle, brought up his own gun and fired again. The slug took the other in the neck, high up and he screamed thinly as he went back in the saddle, his body jerking as if he had been slammed in the chest by an invisible fist. Rob did not give him a second glance. The cattle were stirring restlessly, and it needed only one slight jolt now, of any kind, to start them running and then all hell wouldn't hold them. He had a creepy feeling about it as he urged his mount right up to the lunging, snorting beasts. For the moment, the rest of the rustlers were forgotten. They had to keep the herd milling aimlessly, so that none of the natural leaders would be able to start a breakout. Needle-tipped horns swung at him, ripped through his clothing, missing the flesh of his leg by less than an inch.

Soon, the herd was moving, slowly but surely, breaking up around the perimeter, bawling in loud-throated protest at the heavens. More gunfire echoed around the rim of surging, straining animals. The smell of gunpowder hung thickly in the air as the bellowing rose to a crescendo of sound. Rob's horse wheeled and leapt clear of the swinging horns. Mad beasts lunged this way and that. Gunfire raged all around the milling herd, but there was no stampede.

Leaving Luke, Rob swung his horse, rode back to where a gunfight still raged around one of the camp fires. He wet his lips and fired at a tall man who came racing up on his horse, saw the other teeter in the saddle, hit bad but not killed. Somehow, the wounded man made it away from the fireglow, back into the darkness, no longer a menace.

'They're breaking off towards the hills.' Rob recognized Ovenden's harsh voice, swung in the saddle. A small group of the rustlers, possibly now more than half of their original number were running their mounts back to the shelter of the hills.

Rob followed swiftly, his body straight and tense in the saddle, eyes ranging ahead of him, picking out the individual riders as they swung for the low foothill range. It had been madness for these men to turn and expose their backs like that but panic could do strange things to a man, could make him forsake all reason and now all these men wanted was some kind of shelter from the flying bullets which had so sadly depleted their ranks. They had ridden into a trap of their own making and now it was essential that they should find some way out.

The hoofbeats of his horse was a drumming thunder in his ears as he put his mount to the upgrade path which led up into the hills, where he and Luke had lain in wait for the rustlers. He did not look back as he rode, raking rowels across his mount's flanks, but he knew that other men were riding up at his heels. When he was close enough behind the last man he shot the other's horse from under him, rode up swiftly as the rider fell, arms and legs flailing helplessly as he hit the hard ground. Instinctively, Rob lowered his gun for the killing shot, then eased his pressure on the trigger, noticing even in the faint light that the other was dead, his neck broken by the shuddering impact of the fall.

The other men were riding hell for leather along the winding trail which twisted up the steep hillside. A scatter of shale came down on to Rob's head and shoulders as he reached the treacherous upgrade. There came a harsh yell from the darkness in front of him. Glancing up swiftly, he saw one of the men struggling with his horse. In his hurry to get away, the rider had gone a little too close to the edge of the upgrade, had now seen his danger and was striving mightily to pull his horse away from the side. Almost, he made it.

Then one of the horse's rear legs missed its footing. There came a second wild, high-pitched scream as horse and rider went over the edge, plummeting down a fifty foot drop on to the knife-edged rocks immediately below.

Rob stopped at once. There was little chance now of catching up with the two remaining members of the outfit. They had too big a lead on him and in the darkness there was the chance that he might go the same way as that poor devil who had fallen to his death a few moments earlier. He sat very still in the saddle, feeling reaction beginning to set in. His legs held an old, familiar tremor and he sucked in great gulps of air, rubbing his eyes with the knuckles of his left hand. There was the sharp clatter of hoofs at his back and he turned to see three other men ride up to him. They halted immediately as they saw him.

'What happened?' grunted Ovenden sharply. He leaned forward to peer closely at Rob.

'I dropped one of 'em,' Rob said. He jerked a thumb back along the trail. 'At least, the fall killed him when I shot his horse from under him. Another of them just went over the edge of the trail up yonder.'

'And the others?'

'There were two of 'em. No use goin' up into the hills after them now. They'll have reached the summit and be on their way down. I doubt if you'll be troubled by them again though. They'll just keep on riding, not stopping until they're over the border into Utah.'

Ovenden seemed on the point of saying something more, then he closed his teeth with a snap. After a moment's pause, he said: 'I guess you're right. We've broken this outfit for good.'

'Any of the others alive back there?' Rob asked. He nodded in the direction of the line camp.

'A couple have been wounded. We'll take them back into town and hand them over to the sheriff. I reckon they'll hang for their part in the rustlings.'

They wheeled their mounts and rode slowly back, out of the hills and down on to the lush grass of the valley. The two wounded men were standing by the fire when they rode in. Rob eyed them closely from beneath lowered lids. These were the wild ones, he thought inwardly, there was no mistaking them. He recognized the type only too well. Men who sold their gun to the highest bidder, or joined any outlaw band in the territory that offered them both the excitement they craved for and the money they needed. Few of them ever lived to spend any of the ill-gotten gains.

'We'll head back to the ranch,' said Ovenden quietly. 'I'll leave a handful of men with the herd. The rest of you ride with me. Bring these two men with you. Their mounts should be somewhere around.'

The wounded men were thrust into the saddle, sullen-eyed, lips drawn back as spasms of pain rocked their bodies. Rob could guess at the short trial they would get, if there was any trial at all. They had been caught redhanded and all the evidence any jury needed to convict them was there for anyone to see.

★   ★   ★

It was almost dawn when they topped the low rise which overlooked the Triple Diamond ranch. A pale grey light was stealing through the trees on top of the hill and down below, on one of the slopes, the cattle were beginning to stir. Rob sat easily in the saddle, although there was a deep and growing weariness in him. They rode into the yard, herding the two prisoners in front of them. Two men stepped out of the long shadows, came forward.

'Get your horses from the corral,' Ovenden ordered and threw a gesture of his right hand towards the two men, 'and take these *hombres* into town to the sheriff. Tell him that the hill outfit has been smashed and that these are two of the rustlers. He'll know what to do with 'em, I reckon.'

They sat their mounts, until the four men had ridden on west, the dust kicked up by their horses settling slowly to the still dawn air. Then Rob lowered himself stiffly from the saddle, pulled the cinch loose, laid the trappings on the rail and let his mount go into the corral.

Rose Ovenden came to the door of the house, one arm upraised against the wooden upright. There was a strange look on her face and her eyes were troubled as they fell on Rob. He walked forward, feeling an odd tightness in him which was compounded of a strange fear and apprehension.

'Someone's been here,' said the girl tightly.

Jeff Ovenden said harshly: 'You know who it was, daughter?'

She nodded, her voice sank to a lower tone. 'There were five of them, led by a man wearing a marshal's star. He said his name was Jeb Harbinger, that he was looking for a man called Rob Gardner. Wanted to know if we'd seen him or if he'd come here looking for shelter. I told him we'd seen no one, that he could look around the place if he wanted to.'

'So that's it,' said Rob, very softly. 'He's finally got here.'

'Now it's up to you as to what you do,' said Ovenden. His tone was harsh and severe. 'This is the turnin' point, the fork in the trail. What you decide to do now is goin' to shape the rest of your life.'

'Father, you're asking him to go on out there and get himself killed,' broke in the girl. 'There were five of them and by now, they'll be riding into town, telling their story to the sheriff, getting him on their side. He doesn't have a chance against those odds.'

'Your father's right,' Rob said, speaking very slowly and seriously. 'I've been runnin' all the way from Nebraska. And there has to come an end sometime, someplace. I'm not aimin' to run out on you, Mr Ovenden. But I'll have to head into town and settle this once and for all. If I have to face these five men then that's the way it will have to be.'

'I'd send some of the boys with you if I could,' said Ovenden. 'But — '

'I understand. This is no affair of yours. But you've shown me what I have to do.'

'Better have some rest before you do,' suggested the other. 'Ain't no point in ridin' out like this. You've been up all night and you got very little rest the night before. Harbinger won't mind waitin' another few hours.'

'You've been too good to me already. I'm grateful and I'll pay you back in any way I can.'

'I'll make a bite to eat and then you can rest up until noon,' said Rose quietly. 'Your horse will need a rest too.'

Rob felt too weary to protest. He knew that they were speaking the truth. He would stand no chance at all in his present weary condition. He went inside the parlour with Ovenden. Five minutes later, Rose came in with a tray piled high with coffee, ham and eggs. Rob ate, then rolled his smoke and sat back. The breakfast had acted as a stimulant to him but the smoke relaxed him again and when he went over to the bunkhouse, he was able to pull off his jacket, pants and boots and drop back on to the bunk, closing his eyes and falling asleep almost at once.

How long he slept, he didn't know. He woke to a shake on his shoulder and opened his eyes to find the girl bending over him.

'I thought I'd wake you at noon,' she said. 'The rest of the boys are out getting one of the herds ready to drive to the railhead.'

'Thanks for waking me,' he said quietly. He saw the warm beauty of her now, the gentle lines of her mouth, the full red lips and the dark eyes which watched him from beneath generous brows. The nearness of her struck him forcibly and he felt a tightness grow in him he could scarcely control. Tightening his lips, he said: 'I reckon you'd better go now.'

The faint flush on her face heightened her beauty for him. Then he saw her lift her face for a moment and a look of sadness came over her features, touching her eyes and lips. Without another word, she moved away and went outside. He found that she had brought hot water for him and he unrolled his belongings, took out a small mirror and razor and shaved, feeling fresher after he had done so. Washing up, he went outside into the courtyard. The shadows were few and short and the fiery disc of the sun glared down at him from near the zenith.

A few moments later, Luke came over. The other said: 'I heard about what happened last night while we were away. I want to say that when you first rode here I didn't believe a word you said about this killer marshal on your tail, huntin' you down for somethin' you never did. Now I do.' There was a grim expression on his face. 'These hills and especially the town is full of shadows for a man like you. Kill that marshal and you'll never be the same man again. Go back east and keep on riding until you've worked this out of your system and you feel like a man ought to feel.'

Rob shook his head slowly. 'It's far too late for that,' he said soberly. He gave the other an open, surprised look. 'Why do you reckon I ought to go on runnin'? Surely that's not the sort of life a man should lead?'

'It is if you want to stay alive. A man can never go over the same piece of his life twice, but he can always take the turning that will bring him back on to the right trail again.'

'No.' Rob was adamant. 'This time, I've made up my mind. For some reason, Harbinger wants to take back a dead man and say to the folk in Twin Creeks that this is the killer who murdered the bank guard, that the case is officially closed and he's done his job once more. But he ain't goin' to shoot me in the back like he did most of the others. He'll have to face me like a man.'

'And if you kill him? What then? Will you still go on runnin' from the law. Folk don't take too kindly to anyone who shoots down a marshal.'

'Seems to me that Ovenden thinks otherwise as far as Harbinger is concerned.'

The foreman shrugged: 'That's as maybe. But it's only his opinion. He could be wrong and he ain't the law around here. If Harbinger has got a warrant duly signed by a judge, you ain't got a leg to stand on if you shoot him down, even in fair fight.'

'I'll take that chance.' Going over to the corral, Rob whistled up his horse, threw the saddle on to it, fastened the lashing of his riata, then stepped up, looking down at the other.

Luke paused, chewed on his lower lip for a moment, then said: 'I'll ride in with you Rob. I got no likin' for a man like Harbinger myself.'

Rob shook his head. 'This is my fight,' he said, his tone stern, sharper than he had intended. There was stubbornness in him and something else. All of the anger, the exhaustion, the desires and the great loneliness that had been with him on that long trail from Nebraska, were now channelled and concentrated on one thing, the need for vengeance on the man who had perpetrated these inflictions. He would exact from Harbinger the ultimate in justice. Once that was done, he was prepared to take the consequences. 'I'll go it alone,' he said, 'but thanks for the offer.'

He wheeled his mount with a sharp, vicious twist of the reins. The horse bucked and sunfished in the easy movements of an animal that was glad to be alive. On the point of riding out, he saw Rose Ovenden come down on to the porch. She stood looking across at him, her eyes shaded from the glare of the sun, then walked down into the dusty courtyard, came up to where he sat, tall and grim. She glanced at Luke obliquely.

'Better be about your chores, Luke,' she said.

The other paused, then nodded. 'Yes, Miss Rose.' He backed off, walked with a shambling gait to the bunkhouse, went inside, the door closing after him.

'Do you have to do this, Rob?' Rose looked up at him, troubled for him, angry with him and yet curiously drawn to him.

'It's something which has to be done,' he said harshly. 'I don't like doin' it, but it's either that or keep on runnin' for the rest of my life. Somebody has to face up to this killer who hides behind a badge.'

'Do you suppose they'll let you get out of that town alive?' Her voice stiffened. 'There are five of them, and the four men in the posse looked to be as vicious killers as Harbinger is. They knew I was lyin' when I said you hadn't been here even though they didn't find you when they searched the place. But they know that now you're cornered, you'll either turn and fight or run again. Either way is going to suit them perfectly.'

'I've got to go into town. That's all there is to it.' His tone was final. He had ceased to smile.

'All right then.' She flung the words at him, hitting him with her irritation, and her fear for him. 'Go on into Salenna if you want to. Don't expect me to feel sorry when they kill you.' Her tone and the look at the back of her dark eyes belied the sentiment behind her words. Acting on sudden impulse, he bent low from the saddle, laid his right hand under her chin, lifting it, tilting her face up to him and kissed her full on the lips. He felt the tautness and the anger dissolve out of her, felt the heat and warmth that came out of her. Then she stepped back, touching her lips with her fingers, her eyes still troubled.

'I'll come back,' he said confidently.

'Don't worry for me.' Touching spurs to the horse, he headed out of the courtyard, up to where the hills rolled in a seemingly never-ending sea of green verdure.

He made a wide circle of the hills, keeping clear of the narrow trail which went arrow-straight through them. When he reached timber he traced his way to the main road again, keeping it in sight, but staying back in the undergrowth himself where he could not be spotted from below.

The thought of these five men somewhere in Salenna disturbed him now. Would they have split up, be waiting for him to ride in, or would they be together in one bunch, ready to shoot him down without a chance? The silence of the hills evoked the deep bubbling restlessness in him and he forced himself to think of other things. He thought of Rose Ovenden as he cut down through the trees, and the tension eased a little. In its place there came a feeling of warmth and satisfaction, of something new he had discovered, something he did not want to lose. A woman like that could bring happiness to any man, he reflected. Then, in spite of himself, his thoughts drifted back to Harbinger and a little finger of ice traced a shivering line up and down his spine.

Ten miles or so from the Triple Diamond ranch, the nature of the ground changed. The greenness went and there was arid desert, the ground hard, a desolation stretching towards the dark smudge on the horizon which he took to be Salenna. Under the fierce sun, the heat burning his back and shoulders, he rode at a slow pace, lips tight against the sand, the dust, the sunlight, reflected off the bridle, narrowed down to a needle point of light which hurt the eyes whenever he looked at it. The light hurt him in a strange way, boring into his head, bringing a hurt to his brain. He was riding to kill a man, perhaps five men, and what disturbed him most was the knowledge that he was going to enjoy what he had to do. There was no feeling of sorrow that he was to take the lives of these men. And as for Harbinger himself, he was going to watch death approach him slowly and inexorably, knowing that for him there could be no escape.

The four men who still rode with him were as guilty as he, had the same outlook on life, the same casual disregard for the lives of the men they hunted, the same attitude towards the guilt or innocence of their victims. He wondered for a moment when the rest of the posse had left Harbinger, running out on him somewhere along the trail. Maybe they had had enough of the sheer brutality and ruthlessness of the man. Maybe they had had doubts as to his own guilt and did not like the idea of shooting down an innocent man. Whatever the cause, they had not followed him this far and the odds against him had shortened appreciably.

The sun was still high, the sky unclouded as he left the timber. Now there was nothing here to lessen the heat, no shade, no wind, no water. Sweat poured down his forehead, trickled down his cheeks, mixing with the dust, forming it into a mask that tightened on his flesh as the hours went by. Salenna still seemed as far off as ever and by lifting himself up in the saddle, he was able to make out where tall rough country blocked the trail from this direction. What he had taken to be Salenna, was in reality this stretch of rocky country, guarding the town from the east. He cast a swift glance over the rocks. It was just possible these men might have figured on ambushing him, and this would undoubtedly be the best place to do it.

7

Showdown at Salenna

Jeb Harbinger rode into Salenna shortly before eleven o'clock and made his way to the sheriff's office, dismounting in front of the steps and climbed up on to the boardwalk, walking with the stiffness of many days in the saddle. Opening the door, he went inside, the four possemen crushing in at his back.

Sheriff Heskett dropped his feet from the desk on to the floor, pushed back his chair and got heavily to his feet. For a moment, a startled expression fled across his broad features, then his eyes narrowed just a shade as recognition showed in them.

'Harbinger,' he said, making it something of a question. He nodded. 'I figured you'd be here sooner or later, heard over the telegraph that you were on the trail of some *hombre* named Gardner.'

'That's right.' Harbinger nodded, jerked a thumb towards the four men who lounged near the door. 'The boys and me have been close on his trail all the way from Nebraska. We've finally got him pinned down here.'

'In Salenna?'

'Could be.' Harbinger gave a tight-lipped smile. 'We called at the Triple Diamond place during the night, thought he might be there.' A pause, then: 'What do you know of the man who runs that place, Sheriff?'

'Who — Ovenden? Seems a decent enough man to me. Never had any trouble with him as far as the law's concerned. Could be that some of his hands have got a record someplace, but so long as they don't make trouble around Salenna, I take little notice of that.'

'That could be a dangerous attitude, couldn't it?' There was a little snap to the marshal's voice. He lowered his huge bulk into a chair, resting his hands on the sides, the tiny black hairs on his wrists glistening in the sunlight which slanted through the dusty window.

'How do you figure that?' asked Haskett stiffly. His face said plainly that he did not like the marshal's attitude, riding into town and asking questions in this manner.

'Let's put it this way, Sheriff. I've been huntin' this killer across nearly a thousand miles of country, finally trackin' him down here. Now it could be that this rancher Ovenden has hired him, even though he knows he's got a shady past. You figure that's a good thing, just so long as he doesn't give you any trouble. Because there's a dead bank guard back in Twin Creeks to say different.'

Haskett allowed himself a grim smile. He rummaged about in a drawer of his desk, finally located the piece of paper he was looking for and tossed it across to Harbinger. 'Could be that this may change your mind about that, Marshal,' he said harshly. 'That's a telegraph message I got five days ago. As you'll see, they've caught up with the real killer in Arizona. Seems you've had your sights on the wrong man all the time.'

Harbinger's face was grim, terrible to see, as he stared down at the slip of paper between his fingers. Then he screwed it up into a tight ball, crushing it in his fist, the knuckles standing out whitely with the pressure he was exerting. The veins of his neck protruded under the tanned flesh. After a moment, he said in a voice that was so strained as to be virtually unrecognizable: 'This could be a forgery. You've got no proof that the sheriff in Arizona actually sent this. Anybody can send off a telegraph, even Gardner. It would be one way of savin' his life.'

Haskett shrugged his shoulders. His eyes narrowed down. 'I believe what it says,' he muttered. He threw a quick glance at the men standing near the door, noticing the looks of indecision on their faces. Only the half-breed, standing a little apart from the others did not appear to be concerned by this new piece of evidence.

'I'd say that all of the evidence points towards this man Gardner bein' innocent of this charge,' Haskett went on firmly.

'Then why did he run like that if he was innocent?' demanded Harbinger.

Haskett raised his brows a little. 'When anybody hears that you're on their trail, and that there's maybe some trumped up witnesses to a murder, he ain't goin' to stop and ask himself if he ought to stick around, knowing that he's innocent. There have been too many innocent men shot down by lawmen, or strung up from the handiest tree by a lynch mob. Once it's discovered they're not guilty, it's a little too late to do anythin' about it.'

Harbinger got stiffly to his feet. Anger showed on his face, the veins purpling under the skin. His hands were clenched into tight, rock-hard fists.

'I came out here to take that man back,' he thundered. 'And by God, that's what I aim to do.'

Haskett thinned his lips. 'I don't want any trouble here in Salenna,' he said harshly. 'I'm the law here and none of my men will help you. Not now that I've received this.' He picked up the telegraph message and spread it out with his fingers.

The Marshal glared at the sheriff for a long moment, then turned and stormed out of the office, yelling at the four men: 'Let's get out of here. Seems to me it's too damned easy to hoodwink the law in this town.'

Outside in the street, they mounted up, looking at each other. Harbinger saw the looks, said thinly: 'Well, what are you lookin' like that for? Surely you don't believe him? We'll stay around here. My guess is that soon, Gardner is goin' to come ridin' into town and when he does, we'll be ready for him.'

His lips drew back in a vicious grin, showing his teeth. 'And if that tin-pot lawman tries to stop us, he'll find himself in more trouble than he bargained for.'

'Count me out,' said Adams harshly. He ran the tip of his tongue over his lips. 'I've been thinkin' about Gardner all the time we've been on the trail. I reckoned you were right at first, especially since he continued to run. Now, I know different. We came through no big towns all the way along the trail. There was no place there where he could've sent off a message. Haskett reckons he got that five days ago. Gardner would've been out in the desert then.'

'You tryin' to find some evidence against him bein' guilty?' asked Harbinger, his voice very soft. 'I say he's guilty — as guilty as hell.'

'And I say he's innocent,' retorted Adams. 'If you want to gun him down, you'll do it without me. I want no part of murder.'

Harbinger sucked in a sharp breath, then whirled on the other men. 'Anybody else feel the same way?' None of them answered. Only Morando grinned tightly. 'Let him go, Marshal. We can take care of Gardner without his help.'

Harbinger hesitated, then nodded. 'Let's get a drink first to wash down the trail dust out of our throats and then we'll make plans.'

Adams watched them ride off along the main street, reining up in front of the saloon on the other side of the street, the batwing doors swinging shut behind them as they pushed inside. He waited for a moment longer, as if making up his mind on something terribly important to him, then he gigged his horse, walked it along the street towards the edge of town before digging in spurs, riding back along the trail they had ridden only a few hours before.

★   ★   ★

Rob approached the high rocky ledges cautiously, listening for the faintest sound that might warn him of the presence of other horses. He watched his own mount, knowing that it would pick out anything long before he did, that its senses were far better than his own. He found a kind of trail, moved forward along it until outcropping stopped him, forced him to climb. Loose rocks and slate moved under his horse's hooves but they managed to work their way for close on fifty feet up the steep side of the rise before reaching a level stretch of ground. Now, looking below him, he was able to see where the rocks fell away to the west and it was just possible to make out Salenna in the distance, perhaps seven or eight miles away. The sun was down from its highest point now and there were long, huge shadows among the rocks, giving a thousand places where a man with a high-powered rifle might hide to take a shot at him. He moved over some of the roughest ground he had ever known before coming to the downgrade to where a broad track led through the rocks.

Rock walls glared down at him on either side, throwing a strangely diffuse light into the canyon. Then, as he rounded a bend in the trail, he came upon the man seated on his mount in the middle of the trail, lining up on the other's chest, finger tightening on the trigger, needing only the quick snap of the wrist to bring the sights to bear and send the bullet homing on the target. He had already recognized the other as one of the possemen from Twin Creeks. A man named Adams.

'Hold it, Gardner,' shouted the other harshly. He made no move towards the guns in their holsters. 'I'm here to warn you.'

'Lift your hands over your head,' Rob said harshly. 'And no tricks.'

Slowly, the other raised his hands. Sweat had formed a glistening film on his grim features and he looked scared.

'If you've somethin' to say, better spit

it out — and fast.'

'Harbinger, he's waiting for you in Salenna with the others. They're plannin' to kill you as soon as you ride in.'

'Tell me somethin' I couldn't have figured out for myself,' said Rob scornfully.

The other nodded his head slowly. 'I reckon I can do that,' he said tightly. 'We went to see the sheriff when we got into town. He's got a message sent through to him from some lawman down in Arizona. Seems they've caught that bank robber who shot the bank guard dead. You're in the clear, Gardner. But it won't help you much. Harbinger knows that, but he's determined to kill you. That's why I rode out here to warn you. I want no part in huntin' down an innocent man.'

Rob regarded the other closely for a long moment, then knew instinctively that he was speaking the truth, that this was no trick. Slowly, he lowered the gun, then thrust it back into its holster. Adams stared down at him for a moment, then lowered his arms, keeping his hands well away from his sides.

'You know what they intend to do?'

Adams shook his head. 'I quit as soon as we'd left the sheriff's office, but Harbinger was warned that he'd better not start any trouble in Salenna. Sheriff Haskett has no liking for him though he may not step in and do anythin' to stop him.'

Rob thought fast, trying to determine what this new information meant as far as he was concerned. Now that Harbinger had been warned by the sheriff that he had been proved innocent of the charge against him, then the other would be acting outside of the law if he tried to hunt him down. He smiled grimly to himself. He could shoot down Harbinger in fair fight without running foul of the law.

'What do you intend to do?' He looked across at Adams.

'I've been thinkin' that over in my mind all the way out from Salenna. I don't like to see a man given the raw deal you've had. I'll ride on back with you and see this thing through from the other side.'

'There are four of them and only two of us,' Rob pointed out.

'But it would halve the odds,' muttered the other. He rubbed the back of his hand over his lips. 'This business you and I are in. It's no good. We're fighting each other like dogs and unless we pull out or do somethin' different, we're goin' to die a dog's death. There's nothin' else for me except to ride back and try to square what I've done already.'

'All right, if that's the way you want it,' nodded Rob. He urged his mount forward, came up beside the other. Together, they rode down from the hills, heading towards the town in the distance.

Reining up on the low ridge which overlooked the town, Rob stared down through narrowed eyes. To the west, the sun was going down in a flash of red flame, lighting up the whole of the sky.

In the lurid glow, Salenna lay half in shadow, a few yellow lights showing in the windows which looked down on to the main street. Like so many other frontier towns, there was only one thoroughfare which merited the name of street. The others were narrow alleys which intersected with it at right angles, cutting into it at regular intervals. A plank bridge crossed the narrow creek which ran across the trail between them and the outskirts of the town. Just beyond it, low-roofed houses squatted on either side of the street in the red dusk. Men drifted out of the dim shadows of the boardwalks and there were several horses tied up in front of the saloons and hotel.

'This is where we start bein' careful,' said Rob softly. He eased the guns in their holsters. They rode down the slope, approaching the town. There was no sound, no wind, only the faint bubbling murmur of the water in the creek as they neared it and then the hollow echoes of their horses on the wooden planks of the bridge.

'You think they'll be watchin' the trail into town?' murmured Adams. He spoke thickly, his face tight.

In the west, the reds were slipping away from the sky, and a deep, water-blue spread over the heavens. The yellow light which cut swathes of brightness into the street seemed stronger now by contrast with the deepening gloom.

'If they have any sense, they'll have at least one man watchin' this trail,' he said. 'Maybe it would be safer to circle around and come in from the other direction. We might be able to take 'em by surprise then.'

'They'll have split up, holin' themselves up someplace on either side of the street.'

Rob nodded. 'We'll move around,' he said, making up his mind. They moved along the far bank of the creek, circling the low shacks and broken-down wooden buildings. There were no trees growing close to the town but here and there they came across thickly tangled scrub which afforded them some cover in the growing darkness. Guns ready, eyes alert, searching the shadows, they cut into one of the alleys at the west of town, rode halfway along it, then got off their horses and went the rest of the way on foot, making no sound. A huge rotting warehouse stood on one side of the alley, looming high and dark against the sky. Rob edged towards it, kicked the splintered door in with his boot and slid inside, passing his body close to the rotten woodwork of the wall. The place was empty, filled with the smell of decay and rottenness, the floor covered with a layer of grey dust which had lain undisturbed for years. He backed out into the alley, rejoined the other.

'Not in there,' he stated positively. Carefully, they walked along the whole length of the alley, reached the end where it joined the main street. From here, they were able to see in both directions, out to the very limits of the town.

'There's an empty hotel halfway along the street,' Adams said softly. 'Could be that's where they are. They'll want plenty of room to move around and it's one of the biggest buildings in town.'

'How do you figure we find out if they're there, apart from deliberately exposin' ourselves to their fire?'

'There is no other way,' Adams said hoarsely.

'Place still looks pretty deserted,' muttered Rob.

'It wasn't like this when we rode in this mornin,' Adams said. 'You figure most of the townsfolk are keepin' indoors to be out of the line of fire?'

'That would mean that most everybody knows that this is goin' to happen,' Rob pointed out, 'and you'd reckon the sheriff wouldn't allow that.'

Rob stepped out on to the wide sidewalk, his boots sending hollow echoes into the stillness. The sound of a tinny piano came from one of the saloons, telling them where some of the townsfolk were. It was as good a place as any to stay out of the shooting.

'Somethin' yonder,' said Adams in a strained tone. 'Over by the livery stable.'

Rob switched his glance swiftly. Out of the corner of his vision, he caught the sudden dark movement of shadow inside the open doorway. He listened, then heard the unmistakable click and snap of a rifle lever. He lifted his gun, aimed it at the doorway, edging forward in a half crouch. The man came out into the open a moment later, moving a couple of feet in front of the building, peering intently up and down the street.

'It's Morando, the half-breed,' whispered Adams. He touched Rob's arm.

Rob found his lips dry. He touched them with the tip of his tongue, cast a searching glance along the street, then shouted: 'That's far enough, Morando. Drop that rifle and move over here with your hands lifted.'

For a moment nothing happened,

then the other darted back towards the door of the livery stable, swinging as he moved, aiming the rifle. The bullet knocked wood out of the upright within a couple of inches of Rob's head. Almost without taking conscious aim, he squeezed the trigger, felt the Colt buck in his hand, saw the half-breed take a couple of shambling paces towards the gaping shadow of the door, then throw out his arms and collapse on to his face.

Ducking his head, Rob scuttled swiftly across the darkened street. At any moment, he expected a slug to hit him in the back, but none came and as he threw himself down in the interior of the livery stable, he realized that his luck had held, that the posse had indeed split up, trying to get him one of four ways.

Reaching forward, he turned the half-breed over, felt the limpness as the man flopped on to his back, saw the staring, sightless eyes, and withdrew his hand. 'One down and three to go,' he thought to himself. Worming his way forward, he glanced across the street to where Adams crouched against the boardwalk on the edge of the empty warehouse. He signalled to the other to move forward with him along the street. It was a dangerous manoeuvre, designed to draw the fire of the others.

Eyes alert, he scanned the upper windows of the buildings closely, knowing that it was from here that the others were likely to shoot down on him. He doubted if they knew that Adams had joined up with him and it was possible that they might mistake the other for him, open fire on the man, and give themselves away. The absence of any of the ordinary townsfolk was becoming more and more ominous with every minute of silence. Listening intently, he realized that shortly after the shots had been fired, the music from the saloon had stopped. Now there was a deep and utter stillness lying over the entire town. It was as if an invisible blanket of silence had suddenly dropped over the houses, the saloons and this long street in which only Adams and himself seemed to move, pacing forward on either side of the street, keeping to the deeper shadows, always level with each other.

Still no movement from the buildings. Here and there a stream of light came from an open, uncurtained window, and they were forced to duck beneath it, crawl forward to avoid exposing themselves to gunfire. A shot scattered the silence into shards of sound, sharp echoes that chased each other along the street, atrophying slowly.

Rob spun instinctively as the slug tore wood from the fence nearby. Another shot and he flung himself sideways, but in that same moment he had spotted the bright muzzle flash, knew just where the other man was. He lay still, body stretched out flat on the wooden slats of the boardwalk, holding the Colt firmly in his right hand. He motioned Adams forward with a wave of his other hand, saw the man run from one concealing shadow to another. Ducking down behind a long horse trough, the other opened fire at the window from which the shots had come. Glass shattered, fell from the frames of the windows into the street. Rob caught sight of a shadow that moved swiftly away from the window. Now that the other knew there were two of them, what did he intend to do? The answer to that came less than five seconds later. A rifle shot came from the building less than twenty feet from where Rob lay on his chest. The crash of the shot hammered at his ears and he heard a faint cry come from Adams. Screwing up his eyes, he tried to pick out the other's shape but he had gone down out of sight behind the trough.

Rob edged along the boardwalk until he reached the corner of the building. Two of the possemen were located now. The burning question was: Where was the third man? Moving through the alleys behind him, swinging round to box him in? He glanced over his shoulder instinctively, but nothing moved. By now, the third man would have been alerted by the shots. If it was Harbinger, he would bide his time until he could take him by surprise, shoot him in the back. Harbinger was a gunman, not a gunslinger. He never went into a fight unless he had all of the angles worked out, and the odds were stacked completely in his favour. That was the reason he had stayed alive so long.

Rob gritted his teeth so tightly that an overall ache spread through his jaw and up into his cheeks. This time, Harbinger would not have the advantage of fighting from the shadows. He sighted his gun on the top window opposite, waited for the man to show himself. He did not have to wait long. There came a sudden shout from the lawman on Rob's side of the street and at the same instant, a cracking volley of shots laced across the street towards where Adams lay hidden.

The man behind the top window was

just visible. He had to lean forward a little in order to fire down on Adams and thus exposed himself to Rob's gun. The Colt bucked against his wrist as he aimed it carefully. The shot hammered dust from the edge of the window. Before the man there could pull back, the second slug took him between the eyes, pitching him over the window ledge where he hung for a moment before toppling into the street. His body hit the cover of the boardwalk, crashed through the wood splintering it like matchwood. Hitting the edge of the boardwalk, he rolled into the dusty street, lay still in a patch of yellow lamplight.

'Keep me covered Adams,' Rob yelled harshly. 'While I smoke out this other *hombre*.'

For a moment there was silence and he began to fear that the other had been killed or badly wounded by that earlier shot. Then the other's voice reached him faintly: 'All right Rob. But watch yourself.'

'You all right?'

'Hit in the leg. My own fault, guess I should have stayed under cover.'

Rob said nothing more. Scrambling to his feet, he ran forward, hesitated at corners and leapt quickly across openings, keeping his back to the walls whenever he paused. He had located the window from which the shots had come and pressed himself tightly into the wall a couple of feet from it. There was no sound from inside the room and it was possible that the man who had been there had slipped out the back way, rather than stay and fight.

There was a door on his right and he edged towards it quietly, then paused as he heard the distinct click of a chamber being turned. The man inside was reloading his gun. Without hesitation, Rob kicked in the door, and went inside as it swung back, the latch splintered.

The man near the window, swung away sharply, cried out and turned to start shooting. Rob dropped to his knees, flung himself sideways and was in an almost horizontal position when he commenced firing at the other. The man twisted his body sharply, legs bending under him as he staggered back against the wall near the window. He managed to loose off a single shot that sang through the air within an inch of Rob's head and embedded itself with a leaden impact in the wall at his back. Slowly, Rob went forward, his gun levelled on the other. He could hear the man's slow, guttural breathing, knew that he had not been killed outright by the slug. Bending, he grasped the barrel of the revolver still held in the other's hand and pulled it away from the man's fingers. They seemed to lack the strength to retain their hold on the weapon.

'My chest seems on fire,' said the other in a jerky whisper. He lifted his head and stared up at Rob. There was sweat on his forehead, glistening a little in the faint light, and his mouth worked horribly without any further sound coming out. When he was able to speak again, he said: 'It's the big one, isn't it, Gardner?'

'That's right,' Rob said softly. 'All the way through from breastbone to back.'

'I always figured this is how it would happen,' murmured the other. His breathing grew more shallow. 'Was that Adams shootin' from the other side of the street?'

'Yes.'

'So he went over to your side after all.' For a moment there was a touch of humour in the other's failing voice. 'I never thought he'd do it. I reckoned he would ride west and keep on goin'. Seems you can't rely on anybody now.'

'Where is Harbinger? I know he's hidin' out somewhere in town.'

'He's somewhere. He'll shoot you in the back without warnin'.'

'Was that him across the street?'

The other tried to shake his head, uttered a faint gasp. 'That was — Clem Holliday,' he managed to get out. 'What happened to Morando?'

'He's dead,' Rob said simply. He sat

back on his haunches. So Harbinger was still on the loose somewhere, waiting to pick him off from the darkness. He picked cartridges from his belt and reloaded the chambers of his guns. In front of him, the other gave a harsh gasp. His back arched for a moment, then he relaxed and the air went from his lungs in a faint sigh. Rob felt for the wrist. There was no detectable pulse and he felt the inert limpness in the other's arm as he let it fall on to the man's chest.

Getting slowly to his feet, he moved to the door. He thought of Rose Ovenden and the way she had looked at him when he had ridden out of the courtyard of the Triple Diamond ranch. A lot of things had happened since then and it was difficult to believe that it had been only a few hours before. An eternity seemed to have passed since that moment. He had killed men, shot them down in the darkness. Only a couple of feet separated him from the last man he had killed. Now there was only Jeb Harbinger, somewhere out there in the blackness, nursing his desire to kill. Whatever happened tonight, he would not be the same man who had ridden out of the ranch just a little while before.

He paused in the doorway, careful not to expose himself to anyone along the street. For a moment there was silence and then Adams's voice reached him from the dark shadows.

'You all right?'

'Yes,' he said back. 'This man is dead. There's only Harbinger to go.'

'You know where he might be?'

'Anywhere I guess.' He ran across the street to where the other lay, went down on one knee beside him. 'How bad is it?' he asked through clenched teeth.

'Bleedin' a lot, and painful, but I don't reckon it's too bad. Just a flesh wound. I reckon the slug must've sliced off the bone.'

'Better stay here and keep your head down. I'm goin' after Harbinger.'

'Be careful. That man's as dangerous

as a rattler. He fights the dirty way. A bullet in the back without warnin'.'

'I'll watch out for him. Fortunately it looks as though all of the other citizens are keepin' off the streets.'

Moving forward, he edged his way along the wall of an old assayer's office, across the dark, gaping mouth of an alley that stretched away into blackness towards the far outskirts of town. The place was now as silent as a tomb and he felt a grim tightness in him. He could visualize Harbinger somewhere in the stillness, waiting for him to show himself. The other might have guessed by now that his three companions were dead, that there were only the two of them now, two shadows stalking each other in the darkness and the silence of Salenna.

Pressing his shoulders against sun-whitened wood, he waited. The silence drew out and grew long, but as he waited he remembered all of those long days and nights on the trail, he remembered the fact that Harbinger had known he was hunting down an innocent man, and the knowledge made stone of him, chilling him, giving him the patience to outwait the other. It was waiting that was going to break down Jeb Harbinger.

He heard at last, the faint movement of a horse about thirty yards along the street, switched his glance in that direction, moving only his eyes. There were two horses tethered in front of one of the buildings there and as he watched, he saw that there was a narrow alley joining the street at that point. The horse moved again, kicking its legs in the dust, jerking its head from side to side on the end of the tethering rope. That was the way a horse would act if there was a man somewhere down that alley; moving stealthily forward, anxious to make no sound.

Rob listened carefully, picking out faint night sounds now. Then he heard a stone move, the scrape of a boot on hard earth. Still no sign of the other, but Rob knew now that he was there. A minute passed, then he saw the faint bulge of shadow at the mouth of the alley. The shape eased itself around the corner, not moving away from the wall. Rob heard the scrape of Harbinger's body on the rough wood there and when he heard it he drew up his gun slowly, making no hasty moves which could be seen by a man watching every shadow in the street. Harbinger was around the corner now and both horses were quiet.

At last, he heard a thin sigh come out of the other. It was this need for air which had betrayed Harbinger. He could possibly have picked off the other there and then, but it was not in him to shoot down a man from cover, even a man such as Harbinger. He waited for a moment longer, then said softly:

'Hold it right there, Harbinger. I came here to finish this. Step out into the street and we'll do it properly.'

There came the flash of muzzleblast from the darkness as the other fired, aiming for his voice. The bullet hit a wooden post, whined off into the darkness. 'This is good enough for me, damn you, Gardner,' hissed the other. His tone was hard and strained with tension.

Rob listened to the sound carefully. The other had moved back a little, was edging into the alley once more. He swung a little, watching for the other to expose himself against the sharply-angled corner of the building. He guessed that Harbinger, in attempting to keep him pinned against the wall, had forgotten that he would be forced to expose himself once he began to pull back.

There was a long pause, then he saw the shadow move, aimed and fired. The bullet splintered through wood, the shadow vanished and he knew that he had missed his target. Swiftly, recklessly, he ran forward, cat-footing it over the boardwalk, his Colt held tightly in his fist, finger bar-straight on the trigger. The horses began to thresh again, jerking on the tethering ropes.

He ignored them, reached the corner and peered carefully around it. The alley stretched away in front of him like a river of midnight, still and quiet. Here there were no patches of light to make his man move across so that he could get a snap shot at him. But he was silhouetted against the lighter background of the street and threw himself to one side just in time as gunfire lashed at him from the blackness. Two sharp stilletos of flame lanced at him and he heard the sing of the bullets off the wall nearby as he went down on one knee, jerking up his own gun, levelling it at the muzzleblasts and squeezing off a couple of shots. The burned powder bloomed in a spread of blue-crimson in the darkness. In a second, there came more quick explosions from along the alley. He fired five times and somewhere in the middle of the hammering, thudding racket, he heard his man shout up a loud cry and there came the unmistakable sound of a falling body. A can crashed over on to its side and then rolled with a noisy clatter over the stones.

The stink of powder swirled around Rob as he leaned against the wall, one hand resting on the rough surface. He remained there with a deep, cold patience, waiting to put in the killing shot as he picked out the shallow, stuttering sound of the other's harsh breathing.

Slowly, when no more gunshots sounded, he went forward, balanced carefully on the balls of his feet, ready for a trap, ready to throw himself to one side, but there was nothing like that and a moment later, his foot touched the limp, yielding flesh on the ground in front of him. Bending, he felt the other's body, heard the man groan. Then his fingers touched something warm and sticky.

'Damn you, Gardner,' hissed the other. 'You were the only one I couldn't fight.' A pause, then: 'Ever kill a man before tonight?'

'No,' replied Rob quietly. He sucked

in his cheeks. 'But I've got no regrets about this night's work. It was something that had to be done. If I hadn't done it, there would have come a time when somebody else stopped runnin' and turned to fight.'

'How'd you manage to kill the others?'

'You forgot about Adams. There was a man with a conscience. He rode back to warn me of what you meant to do, also that you knew I was innocent of killin' that bank guard. Guess he wanted to do somethin' to wipe out the knowledge of what he did when he followed you, so he came back with me.'

'Damn fool!' muttered the other throatily. 'I ought to have known better than to let him go. I ought to have shot him down there and then.'

The marshal had been stirring slowly on the rough stones of the alley. Now he suddenly twisted and then lay still in the darkness. Rob touched him, shaking him with his hand, felt the lumped looseness of the man under his fingers and knew that Jeb Harbinger had ridden the trail after his last prisoner. He thought of all the other men this man had hunted down, shooting them in the back so that he might take them back dead and acting on impulse, he caught hold of the marshal's badge pinned to the other's shirt and ripped it off with a sharp tug. The other's shirt tore as he did so. Slipping the silver badge into his pocket, he got to his feet, walked slowly out of the alley and into the street, heading for the sheriff's office. He was nursing an odd feeling, one which he could not define. Pushing open the door of the office, he stepped forward into the yellow lamplight. The man with the star, seated behind the desk, glanced up at him, then down at the bloodstained badge which Rob had tossed on to the desk.

'Rob Gardner,' said Sheriff Haskett, his voice expressionless.

The other nodded slowly.

Haskett eyed him steadily for a

moment, then said slowly: 'I've been expectin' you.' He got to his feet, walked over to the far side of the room, came back a moment later, with a bottle and a glass. Pouring the whiskey into the glass, he pushed it across the desk to Rob. 'Better drink that down,' he said. 'You look as though you could use it.'

For a moment, Rob looked at the other in surprise, then the sheriff gave a brisk nod. 'I know all about what's been happening to you since Harbinger started out on your trail from Nebraska. I know that you're innocent of that charge he made against you and I know that there ain't nothin' the law can do to you for what you did tonight. I see it only as self-defence. I even went so far as to warn Harbinger of the consequences if he tried to arrest you.'

'Then you're not arrestin' me?' asked Rob.

Haskett smiled thinly, shook his head. 'I'll have one of my deputies bring in the bodies.'

'There's a wounded man out there too. His name is Adams. He was with Harbinger, but he rode out to warn me and then came back into town with me.'

'I'll see the Doc takes a look at him,' promised the other. 'As for you, my advice is to get a good night's sleep and then ride back to the Triple Diamond. I've an idea you're needed there.' His smile widened. 'Not just by Jeff Ovenden, either. Time somebody tamed Rose Ovenden, maybe you're the one to do it.'

THE END